All Andie wanted to do now was go home....

Go home to her apartment and close all the blinds and sit on her bed and hug the tattered old teddy bear that she'd had since she was a child.

Clay had *kissed* her.

A *real* kiss. A man-and-woman kiss.

It wasn't possible. But it was true.

And, Lord forgive her, she had *liked* it. Liked it more than any kiss she'd ever had in her life.

And then, after that incredible, unforgivable kiss, he'd told her he wanted to *marry* her.

Marry her....

All her life she'd thought that watchful, cautious Clay was like a sleeping volcano. Now and then she'd wondered what it would be like if he woke up someday and started spewing fire.

Well, now she knew....

Dear Reader,

Welcome to Silhouette **Special Edition**...welcome to romance.

In this festive month of December, curl up by the fire with romantic, heartwarming stories from some of your favorite authors!

Our THAT SPECIAL WOMAN! title for December is *For the Baby's Sake* by Christine Rimmer. Andrea McCreary's unborn baby needed a father, and her decision to marry friend Clay Barrett was strictly for the baby's sake. But soon, their marriage would mean much more to them both!

Lisa Jackson's LOVE LETTERS series continues this month with *C Is for Cowboy*. Loner Sloan Redhawk is hot on the trail of his prey—a headstrong, passionate woman he won't soon forget! Also returning to **Special Edition** in December is reader favorite Sherryl Woods with *One Step Away*.

Rounding out this holiday month are *Jake Ryker's Back in Town* by Jennifer Mikels, *Only St. Nick Knew* by Nikki Benjamin and *Abigail and Mistletoe* by Karen Rose Smith.

I hope this holiday season brings you happiness and joy, and that you enjoy this book and the stories to come. Happy holidays from all of us at Silhouette Books!

Sincerely,

Tara Gavin
Senior Editor

Please address questions and book requests to:
Silhouette Reader Service
U.S.: 3010 Walden Ave., P.O. Box 1325, Buffalo, NY 14269
Canadian: P.O. Box 609, Fort Erie, Ont. L2A 5X3

CHRISTINE RIMMER

FOR THE BABY'S SAKE

Silhouette®

SPECIAL EDITION®

Published by Silhouette Books
America's Publisher of Contemporary Romance

For my friend, Vilma Roth Rakosi.
Oh, the times we had.
Is it a miracle we lived to tell about them?
Probably.
But we did. And we do.

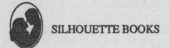 SILHOUETTE BOOKS

ISBN 0-373-09925-8

FOR THE BABY'S SAKE

Copyright © 1994 by Christine Rimmer

CHRISTINE RIMMER

is a third-generation Californian who came to her profession the long way around. Before settling down to write about the magic of romance, she'd been an actress, a sales clerk, a janitor, a model, a phone sales representative, a teacher, a waitress, a playwright and an office manager. Now that she's finally found work that suits her perfectly, she insists she never had a problem keeping a job—she was merely gaining "life experience" for her future as a novelist. Those who know her best withold comment when she makes such claims; they are grateful that she's at last found steady work. Christine is grateful, too—not only for the joy she finds in writing, but for what awaits when the day's work is through: a man she loves who loves her right back and the privilege of watching their children grow and change from day to day.

OREGON

NEVADA

Meadow Valley
•

★ Sacramento

San Francisco
•

Monterey
•

CALIFORNIA

Santa Barbara
•

Los Angeles
•

Palm Springs
•

San Diego
•

PACIFIC OCEAN

MEXICO

All underlined places are fictitious.

Chapter One

Clay Barrett watched his cousin, Andie McCreary, push her food around on her plate. He knew she was trying to make it appear that she was eating, but he wasn't fooled. He'd also noticed that she'd refused both wine and a cocktail.

"Everything all right?" their waitress asked.

Andie shot the waitress a smile, one that tried its best to be bright. "It's wonderful. Thanks." Then she bent her head earnestly over her plate and pushed the food around a little more.

Clay cast about for the right opening. "You know, it's worked out surprisingly well, your running the office. I'll be frank. I didn't expect it to."

Andie looked up at him, her brown eyes unnervingly direct. "I know you didn't. You let me stay on when you took over because Uncle Don asked you to give me a chance."

Her frankness surprised him a little, but he recovered quickly and admitted in a cautious tone, "That's true."

Don and Della Barrett had adopted Clay when Clay was ten years old. The love and gratitude he felt toward them was the cornerstone on which his life was built. There was very little he could refuse either of them.

Andie added pointedly, "But you *kept* me on because I run Barrett and Company better than you ever thought it could be run."

"Right again." Clay tried a smile.

Andie didn't smile back. "I'd be difficult to replace."

"No argument."

Andie caught her inner lip lightly between her teeth. It seemed to Clay that he could hear what she was thinking: *are* you going to replace me?

But she didn't say the words aloud. A few other things still remained to be said first. They hadn't quite worked their way around to those things yet. But they would, very soon now.

Andie concentrated on her plate again. Clay looked at the sleek crown of her head and thought of the past, of their rivalry when they were growing up.

Andie had been the family darling, the *lovable* one, the mere fact of her existence enough to get her anything she wanted. Clay was the achiever. He showed his worth by what he did.

Their resentment of each other had been as natural as breathing. They'd disliked each other on sight, from the day the Barretts had adopted Clay. And they went on disliking each other, right up to the day Clay left home, on full scholarship, for UCLA.

When Clay left, he'd been eighteen and Andie had been seventeen. Clay hadn't come back for ten years, except to visit. But then last April his father had suffered a heart attack. At the family's urging Clay had decided to return right away to Northern California to take over his father's one-man accounting and investment-consulting firm.

When Clay stepped in at Barrett & Co., his cousin Andie had been the office manager there for two years. Clay had been absolutely positive that he and Andie wouldn't last a week as a team.

He'd been dead wrong. In the years that Clay had been away, his willful, unfocused cousin had grown up.

Clay was stunned to discover that Andie was absolute dynamite at her job. She could work circles around any of the topnotch clerks and secretaries he'd used in L.A. at the major international firm where he'd been clawing his way up through the ranks for five years.

Andie kept ahead of the work load. She was pleasant and businesslike. The clients adored her. And if she remembered how she and her new boss used to squabble and fight when they were teenagers, she never mentioned it or let it affect their working relationship.

Yes, it *had* worked out. It was still working out, in spite of the change in Andie the past couple of months.

Andie pushed her plate away, giving up the pretense that she would eat the food on it.

The waitress appeared again. "All done?"

Andie nodded. Clay ordered coffee. The waitress looked questioningly at Andie.

Andie shook her head and murmured, "Nothing more for me."

"You can bring the check, too," Clay said.

The waitress went about her business, pouring Clay's coffee and bringing the bill. Andie fiddled with her water glass and watched the busers and the hostess, the waiters and the other customers, anyone but Clay.

Clay studied Andie, noting, as he was always doing lately, the faint shadows, like tender bruises, beneath her eyes, the grim set to her pretty mouth. She seemed thinner than before, and there was a tautness about her.

At the office, she was as wonderfully efficient as always, maybe more so. But the charm and the openness that Clay had believed as much a part of her as her gleaming nearly black hair and her easy, musical laugh, were gone. For the past several weeks, Andie had burned with a determined kind of heat.

And Clay had to face facts here. It was the end of *February,* for God's sake. Tax time was upon them. Barrett & Co. was enjoying a brisk business. And it was going to keep getting busier until April fifteenth. If Andie flaked out on him, Clay was going to have problems.

And if Clay had problems, his father, who only worked a few hours a day now, would be drawn back into the business full-time. Don didn't need that kind of pressure, not anymore. That kind of pressure could cause another heart attack. And another heart attack might be the end of him.

"I know what you're thinking, Clay." Andie's voice was tight.

Clay realized he'd been silent too long. He looked up at the beamed ceiling overhead.

"God, Andie..." He breathed the words softly and in them he heard all of his own worry and frustration.

"I'm not going to let anybody down," she said slowly and evenly, as if she was afraid he might not understand the words. "I swear to you. I can handle this."

The moment of truth was upon them. He demanded, quietly, "And just what is *this?*"

Her mouth twisted. A spark of anger lit her eyes. All at once, the old rivalry was there again, rising up to poison the air between them.

"You know. Don't pretend you don't." She spoke in a low, intense whisper. "I've seen you watching me lately, *measuring* me, putting that razor-sharp mind of yours to work on the changes in me. We might as well be kids again, the way you've been following me with those eyes of yours."

Clay stared at her, understanding exactly what she meant. When they were kids, he *had* watched her. She was always doing things she shouldn't and he was always finding her out. He'd caught her pawing around in Granny Sid's bureau drawers when she was nine, smoking one of her father's Roi Tans when she was eleven and riding on the back of Johnny Pardo's Harley Davidson when she was fifteen.

"I never ratted on you." The childish words were out of Clay's mouth before he knew he would say them. They were words from the old language they had shared growing up, the language of their rivalry and mutual resentment.

Andie answered in the same vein. "You never had to rat. You knew. You knew *everything*. I hated you for that, for watching and knowing all the ways I messed up, while you were so perfect and did everything right."

"Andie..."

"No." She chopped the air with a hand, then dragged in a breath. Her eyes shone with tears that she wouldn't let fall. She looked up at the beamed ceiling, just as Clay had a few moments ago, as if seeking whatever he had sought there.

At last she lowered her chin and met his gaze across the table. "I'm sorry. I promised myself I wasn't going to do that."

"What?"

She sighed and the saddest hint of a smile tugged the corners of her mouth. "Act like a brat." She waved a hand on which a gold bracelet of delicate linked hearts gleamed.

"Prove to you that I'm still the flaky little twit I was when we were kids."

"I know you're not." He spoke with firm conviction.

She peered at him sideways and in the dim light, for a single instant, she almost looked mischievous. "Meaning I *was* a flaky little twit back then?"

He looked at her, not speaking, realizing he'd more or less put his foot in it.

She echoed his thoughts. "Cautious Clay puts his foot in it once again." She called him by the name she used to taunt him with back in the old days.

He tried to look accusing. "You set me up for that one."

She let out a teasing chuckle. "I certainly did. And it's all right. You only said the truth. I *was* a flaky little twit when we were kids."

"A very charming flaky little twit."

Two spots of color appeared on her pale cheeks. "Well, thank you very much."

"You're welcome." He felt absurdly satisfied to have heard her laugh, to have been the cause of her blush, however faint.

They were quiet for a moment. But it wasn't a bad silence, Clay thought, with some relief. Somehow, resurrecting their old antagonism had reminded them of what their current professional relationship often made them forget.

Beyond being a boss and an employee, even beyond the actual fact of being cousins, they were *family*. They were *connected*—not by blood, since Clay had been adopted—but through the people they both loved and through a shared past.

"Hell. Andie."

"Go ahead. Ask it." The last traces of her teasing laughter had fled. Her eyes were haunted again, her expression resigned.

There was nothing else to do but say it. "Are you pregnant?"

She sighed and rubbed her eyes. "Yes, I am. Are you going to fire me?"

Chapter Two

Clay glared at her, offended. "I wouldn't fire you just because you're pregnant. What do you think I am?"

But Andie didn't want to fight with him. "Clay, don't get self-righteous on me. Please."

He relaxed a little. "All right. Sorry. Let's try this another way."

"What way?"

"Let me start out right now by saying that I have no intention of firing you."

Her slim shoulders slumped, whether with relief or weariness, Clay didn't know for sure. "That's one problem solved," she said softly. "Thank you."

"Don't thank me. I'm the one who should be thankful that you aren't planning to quit. As you pointed out a while ago, you'd be damn near impossible to replace."

"Oh, Clay." Her expression was very vulnerable suddenly. In a totally spontaneous gesture, she reached across the table and squeezed his hand. "Do you have any idea how much it means to me to hear you say that?"

Her hand was warm over his. Clay liked the way it felt, which shocked him a little, for some strange reason. He must have stiffened, because she quickly took her hand away.

"I've embarrassed you," she said in a tiny voice.

He cleared his throat. "No. No, really. You haven't. Not at all." God, he was babbling like an idiot. He drew in a long, slow breath. Then he reminded himself that there were still some things they had to get clear between them.

He made himself ask, though it came out sounding pompous and ridiculously formal. "So then it's settled that you won't be leaving Barrett and Company?"

"Yes."

"Good. So. Are you planning to get married?"

"No."

"I see." He forced himself to go on, though each word emerged more stilted than the last. "Then as far as the, er, child. What exactly do you plan to do about that?"

That burning intensity came into her eyes again. "I'm going to keep it."

He tried to assimilate what she was telling him. "Raise a baby *alone?*"

She let out a little puff of air, then pointed out in a too-reasonable tone, "I'm a single woman. How else would I raise it?"

He knew he should probably just let it be, yet he heard himself asking, "Do you really believe that's the best choice?"

"It's *my* choice." She looked down at the table and then lifted her head again to face him directly. "I've thought about it a lot, Clay, believe me. It's what I want and the best I can do, given the circumstances." She curled her fingers around her water glass, as if to steady herself. Then she shot Clay a defiant look. "A lot of women raise children alone these days."

"That doesn't mean it's a good thing."

"I didn't say it was *good*. I said it's the way it is."

Right then, the hostess led another couple to a booth near theirs. Both Clay and Andie fell silent for a moment, guarding the privacy of their conversation.

As Clay watched the hostess handing out menus, he reminded himself that he really shouldn't get in too deep here. He shouldn't push for answers to questions he was probably better off not thinking about.

He already had most of the information he required as Andie's boss. She was going to be a mother and she wanted to keep working for him. All he needed to know now was how she planned to manage everything—how much leave she was going to need and when she would need it. The rest was her own personal business.

But he couldn't seem to stop himself. Once the other couple was settled with their menus, he turned to his cousin and asked, "What about the father?"

Her shoulders tensed. "What about him? He's not involved."

Clay leaned forward. He pitched his voice low. "Who is he?"

She flinched, then steadied herself. "It doesn't matter."

"Of course it matters."

"No, it doesn't. As I said, he's not involved."

"Andie, I just want to know who he is."

"I understand that." Her jaw was set. "And I'm not going to tell you."

"Why not?"

"Because it's not really any of your business, Clay. And because it would probably only cause trouble if you knew."

"What do you mean, trouble?"

"I mean, you might get it into your head that you should go after the guy or something. I don't know." She lifted her hands in a helpless gesture. "How should I know what you'd do? I just know that nothing but trouble could come from your knowing the man's name."

"That's not necessarily true."

"I don't want to argue any more about this. I'm not telling you. That's all." She had that stubborn, determined look she used to get when they were kids. Whenever Andie got that look, it didn't matter what a guy did, she wouldn't talk.

Clay tried another tack. "Are you saying that the father wants nothing to do with the child?"

Andie sat back from him, then she lifted her water glass and drank from it. Carefully she set down the glass. "Look. What was between me and him just didn't work out."

"Does he *know* that you're pregnant."

"Yes. He knows."

"How did he find out?"

"I contacted him and told him about it."

"And?"

"I told him I thought he should know, that's all."

"What did he say?"

"What could he say? I told you, it was already over between us. There was no chance of trying again, even for the sake of a child. We just . . . aren't suited to each other. But I did tell him about the baby, because it seemed like he had a right to know. And he said he'd help out wherever he could, but he didn't want me to involve him."

Clay's chest felt tight. "And that was it?"

He saw the flicker of hesitation in her eyes before she answered, "Yes."

"What else?"

"Clay . . ."

"Just tell me. What else?"

"You're bullying me."

"What else?"

"All right, all right. He sent some money."

"Money."

"Yes. To help out."

"To help out."

She glared at him. "Is there an echo in here?"

He ignored her sarcasm. "Is he going to give the baby his name?"

Andie looked away, then back. "No. He's not. And that's fine with me."

"But I thought he said he'd help you *wherever he could?*"

"Clay, I—"

"What does that mean, *wherever he could?*"

"Clay, if you don't stop this—"

"Just answer me. What does that mean?"

"I'm not kidding here, Clay."

"He could help you by marrying you. Did he say anything about that?" Clay heard the leashed rage in his own voice. He tried to rein it in. He reminded himself again that the things he was grilling her about didn't really concern him at all. But now that the fact of Andie's pregnancy was out, he was finding it very hard to deal with.

Damn it, she *was* family to him. And she had been used. He just couldn't help imagining the immense satisfaction he'd feel if he could only get his hands on the thoughtless bastard who'd done this to her, the rotten worm who now seemed to think a few lousy bucks would get him off the hook.

Andie was looking at him guardedly.

He asked again, "What about the man doing the right thing and marrying you, Andie?"

"Stop it, Clay."

"Well, what about it?"

"If you don't settle down, I'm going to get up and leave." She spoke softly but very deliberately.

He stared at her. On the table between them, both of his fists were clenched. "I'm sorry." He pushed the words out through his teeth.

She met his gaze, unwavering. "Then relax. Sit back. Take a deep breath or two."

"Fine. I will."

"Good. Then do it."

He closed his eyes and mentally counted to ten. Then he made himself sit back in the booth. He pulled air into his lungs and slowly let it out.

"Better," she said warily.

"Good. Now, what about his marrying you?"

She looked at him for a moment, as if gauging how much to say. At last she allowed, "I told you, it's over between us. It didn't work out. I don't want to marry him. And he doesn't want to marry me."

"Why is that?"

She looked away. "Enough. Stop."

"What?"

"I said, enough. I don't want to talk any more about the father. There's nothing more to say about him. I cashed the check he sent me and that's the end of it. I want nothing more from him. I'm not going to marry him, but I *am* going to raise my baby. The man is out of my—*our*—lives. For good and all."

"There are laws, Andie, that will force the man to take responsibility for—"

She put up a hand. "I don't care about laws. My baby and I will be just fine on our own. We'll manage. If you can't accept that, Clay, then maybe I will have to look for another job."

"More coffee?" The smiling waitress appeared out of nowhere, coffeepot held high.

Clay shook his head tightly. Andie gave the young woman a sheepish smile.

"Well, if you need anything else..."

"We won't," Clay said, not bothering to disguise his impatience. The waitress left them. As soon as she was out of sight, Clay turned to his cousin. "Please don't quit." Somehow he managed a rueful shrug. "I'll do my best to mind my own damn business."

Andie nodded. "Fair enough."

Clay forced himself to stop thinking murderous thoughts about an unknown man and to consider the things they really did have to agree on. "So. Have you figured out how you intend to run my office and also have a baby a few months from now?"

"It's more than a few months away, thank goodness," she corrected him.

"When?"

"I'm due in September. That's seven months."

In his head a voice whispered, *Then she's two months along.*

Which meant she'd probably become pregnant over the holidays.

Over the holidays, while Jeff was here...

"My due date is September twenty-fourth," Andie was saying. "I saw a doctor just last week."

God. He didn't want to think it. But the timing was right.

And Clay had seen the signs that Andie and Jeff were drawn to each other. His best friend and his cousin had spent at least one evening alone together, as a matter of fact.

"Clay?" Andie's voice showed concern. "Are you all right?"

"Fine. I'm fine."

No, he told himself firmly, it wasn't Jeff. It *couldn't* be Jeff. He wasn't even going to let himself imagine a thing like that. He reminded himself for the umpteenth time to mind his own business, to stick to the question of how she planned to manage both a job and motherhood.

"Clay?"

He blinked. "Yes. Now, where were we?"

"Are you sure you're—"

"Absolutely." He answered the question before she finished it, then suggested, "Since you've thought this all through, why don't you tell me exactly what you have in mind?"

She actually smiled as she launched into her plans. "All right. I'd like to work as long as I can and then I'll take a short leave, maybe eight weeks at the most, to have the baby. I intend to be back at the office as soon as I can find a good baby-sitter. It should work out just fine. Or at least as fine as something like this *can* work out. I mean, September isn't a half-bad time, really. Things aren't too crazy then. And I can be back before the first of the year, when it all starts picking up again." She tipped her head and regarded him. "So, how does that sound?"

Superimposed over Andie's features he saw Jeff's face, the laughing blue eyes and the devilish grin.

"Clay?" Andie asked anxiously.

He could hear Jeff's voice, back in college, when a woman Jeff didn't even know threw her arms around him at a homecoming game and kissed him right on the mouth. Jeff had winked at Clay over the woman's shoulder. *Hell, bud. I'm fatal to women. What can I say?*

"Clay, does that sound all right?"

Clay blinked and forced himself back to the here and now. "Yeah, Andie. It sounds just fine. And I'm glad to hear you've been to a doctor, that you're taking care of yourself."

"I am. I promise." She gave him a real smile now, and it occurred to him how much he'd missed her smiles the past few weeks. She shifted in her seat. "So, then. Are we done?"

"One more thing."

"Yes?"

"Your parents—have you told them yet?"

"No."

"When will you tell them?"

"Right away."

"And what will you say?"

"Just what I said to you. That I'm going to have a baby and I'm raising it on my own."

The very next night Andie faced her parents.

She had them over to her apartment on High Street and she cooked them pot roast. Her father loved pot roast.

Andie waited until the dinner dishes had been cleared away and her father was on his second helping of chocolate cake before she dared to broach the subject of the baby.

With her stomach feeling queasy and her heart pounding a little too fast, she got up to refill her parents' coffee cups and took her seat again. Then she folded her hands on the tabletop and gave a little cough, because her throat felt so tight.

"Andie?" her mother asked, before Andie had said a word.

Andie met her mother's dark eyes and saw the worry and apprehension there. The past several weeks, her mother had asked her more than once if something was bothering her. Andie had put her mother off with vague replies. She said she was fine, or that she was a little tired. But her mother hadn't been convinced, Andie knew. And now, with that emotional sixth sense a mother often has, Thelma Mc-

Creary understood that she was on the verge of finding out what had been troubling her only child.

Andie wanted to break down and cry. But she didn't. Now was not the time for indulging herself. Now was the time to tell the truth and tell it with dignity.

As much of the truth as *could* be told, anyway.

She had considered holding off telling them until she was in her second trimester. But last night had changed her mind about that. Somehow, the moment she'd told Clay the truth, she'd seen that there was no point in postponing telling the rest of them. The sooner they knew, the sooner they could start to get used to the idea of having a single mother in the family.

Andie looked from her father to her mother, thinking that there were a lot of women in the world who'd give anything to have a close-knit family as she had. But there was a price to pay for being part of such a family. If she were all alone in the world, she wouldn't have to tell painful truths like this to people whose love and respect she craved. If she were all alone in the world, the fact that she was going to have a baby without being married would be nobody's business but her own.

"Andie, what is it?" Andie's mother had set down her fork, leaving her cake only half-eaten.

"Well, I—"

Her father now pushed his own plate away. "All right. What's going on? Something's going on."

"I think," Thelma said rather faintly, "that Andie wants to tell us something."

"What?" Andie's father demanded. "What does she want to say?"

"Just wait, Joe. Let her get to it." Thelma patted her husband's hand.

The wifely gesture sent a sharp pang through Andie. She thought of the tiny baby that slept within her and couldn't help wishing there was a good man like her father at her side.

But there wasn't. She was on her own. That was reality. And she had made her choice.

Andie straightened in her chair. She forced a smile to meet her parents' worried frowns.

"I don't really know how to go about telling you this. I know you're not going to like it, and that it will probably hurt you. And I'm sorry, so sorry. But I've made up my mind."

"What?" Joe impatiently wiped his mouth with his napkin. "You've made up your mind about what?"

"Oh, Dad . . ."

"What? For God's sake, Andie. Tell us."

"I'm going to have a baby."

There. The words were out.

And Andie felt as if she'd dropped them down a bottomless well.

Her father's face went unhealthily pale. And then beet red. Andie thought of Uncle Don. Of heart attacks and strokes and all the things that happen to men in their late fifties who are a little overweight and a little overstressed and then receive a nasty shock.

Andie looked at her mother. Thelma's eyes were very wide. And then they softened. Great tenderness filled them.

"Oh, honey . . ." Thelma reached across the table, groping for her daughter's hand.

Andie responded without hesitation. She met her mother's hand halfway and was glad for the unconditional love she saw in her mother's eyes.

"You should have told us right away," Thelma whispered.

"I had to have time to think. I had to be sure."

"I know, I know."

"It's what I want, Mom."

"Of course you do."

Suddenly, Joe found his voice. He used it to point out the obvious. "You're not married, Andrea." He was clearly so upset, he'd called his daughter by the name she was born with.

Still clasping each other's hands, both women looked at him.

"Don't you two give me those looks," Joe said with some testiness. "I'm stating a fact, here. You don't have a husband, Andie."

"Now, Joe," Thelma began in her most placating tone.

Andie pulled her hand from her mother's warm clasp. "It's all right, Mom."

"But I—"

Andie drew herself up. "No. It's all right." She faced her father. "You're right, Dad. I don't have a husband."

"Are you *going* to have a husband?"

"Joe..."

"Quiet, Thelma." He narrowed his eyes at his daughter. "*Are* you?"

"Maybe someday, yes."

"What about right now, Andrea? It seems to me a husband is something you could use right away. It seems to me that the father of your baby might be a good choice as that husband, as a matter of fact."

Andie felt her skin going prickly and her heart beating a sharp, erratic rhythm in her chest. She told her body to calm down. She reminded herself that she'd never expected this to be easy.

But having known it wouldn't be easy didn't make her like it. She'd hated seeing the disapproval and concern in Clay's eyes and she hated seeing them in her father's eyes, as well.

"Look, this is *my* baby." She tried to keep her voice from rising out of control. "No one else's. The father isn't involved. I'm going to have it alone and I'm going to raise it the very best I can on my own.''

''Oh, dear,'' Thelma said to no one in particular.

''But a baby needs a father,'' Joe insisted gruffly. ''And what about money? It's only fair that the man—''

''Just drop it, Dad. I mean it. I'll manage, as far as money goes.''

''What about your job? Clay is counting on you to—''

''I've worked things out with Clay.''

There was a tiny pause. Andie saw the flicker of a look that passed between her mother and her father.

Her father said carefully, ''You've talked to Clay about this?''

''Yesterday evening, yes.''

''And what did he say?''

''He said he wants me to keep working for him. So that means I'll be able to support myself and the baby. It won't be easy, but it will certainly be manageable.''

''Well.'' Her father slid a glance at her mother again, then said to Andie, ''At least you still have a job.''

''Yes, I do.''

Joe scrubbed a hand down his broad, lined face. ''Well, that's something. You're lucky there.''

''I am not *lucky* there, Dad. I'm good at my job, and Clay doesn't want to lose me.''

''Well, certainly. Of course. But I still think the father ought to—''

''That's enough, Dad. Really. I wanted you to know the situation, because I love you both and don't want you to be in the dark about something so important. But it's *my* situation. I'll handle it the way I think best.''

''It's crazy.''

''Joe, please . . .''

''No, it's crazy, Thelma. And you know it. Women having babies without a man beside them. It's not right.'' Joe looked at Andie, a weary look.

A look that hurt. It was a look she used to see on his face all the time, back when she was growing up, back when he'd considered her flighty, willful and irresponsible and was always saying he didn't know what he was going to do with her.

In the past few years, Andie knew, her father's opinion of her had changed greatly. He looked at her with pride now, and he often told her how pleased he was that she had finally grown up.

"It will work out," Thelma said, her voice brittle with forced cheer.

Joe shook his head. "Andie, Andie. What are we going to do with you?"

Chapter Three

That Saturday, Clay's father called him and asked him to dinner.

The first thing Clay noticed when he pulled up in front of the house where he'd grown up was that his mother's little four-by-four compact car wasn't in the driveway where she usually parked it. His Uncle Joe's truck, however, was.

Clay knew right then that dinner wasn't the only thing cooking here. He recognized all the ingredients for a "man-to-man" talk.

His uncle and his father were going to pump him for anything he might know about Andie's predicament. He could feel it coming.

Since there was nothing to do but get it over with, Clay left his own truck and went up the front walk past the snowball bush at the front gate. Right now, in the last third of winter, the bush looked like a dead weed.

There were still patches of melting snow in the yard from the last storm a few weeks before. As Clay picked his way around them, the first flakes of a new storm were beginning to fall.

Inside, there was a cheery fire in the new pellet stove Don had put in two years ago. The walls of the living room were pale blue, instead of the light green they used to be when Clay was growing up.

Not much else had changed, though. The same family pictures decorated the walls and the tall vase with the big fake flower arrangement erupting from it still stood beside the front door. Clay hung his heavy jacket in the coat closet and told his dad he'd love a beer.

They settled in the living room. Don and Joe held down either end of the couch. Clay took the wing chair that had been reupholstered in a pattern of blue flowers to complement the walls.

Apprehensive, Clay refused to speak first. As the two older men tried to figure out how to begin, Clay watched them, very much aware of the closeness between them, of their solidarity as long-time members of the same family.

Their wives were sisters and they were best friends. The four of them—Clay's mother, his aunt, his father and his uncle—had grown up together right here in Meadow Valley. And when it had come time to settle down, Don had married Della and Joe had married Thelma. Joe and Thelma had had one child, Andie. And when Della and Don had realized they would have no children of their own, they had set out to adopt a baby.

But then they'd come to understand how many older, less "desirable" children needed families. They'd been introduced to Clay. And they'd taken him to their hearts.

Joe glanced at his brother-in-law. Almost imperceptibly, Don nodded.

Joe shifted a little and adjusted his belt more comfortably under the paunch he'd developed over the past few years. He cleared his throat.

Clay ached to get this over with. He almost volunteered, *It's about Andie, right?*

But he held the words back. What if it *wasn't* about Andie, after all? Then Cautious Clay would have really put his foot in it, but good.

Clay's father, seeing that his brother-in-law couldn't think how to begin, suggested, "We might as well get it right out there, Joe."

Joe looked down at his beefy hand, which was resting on his knee. "I know, I know."

Don reached out and touched Joe's shoulder. "Do you want me to... ?"

Joe nodded. "Yeah, would you?"

Don squared his shoulders and turned his level gaze on his son. "Clay, Andie says she's explained to you about her situation."

Clay looked at his father warily, knowing now that he'd been right all along. It *was* about Andie. Still, he didn't want to reveal anything that she hadn't already disclosed. "What situation?"

"That she's going to have a baby," Uncle Joe said in a rush, as if he had to get it out fast, or it wouldn't come out at all.

Now that it *was* out, Clay allowed himself to nod. "Yes. She's told me."

Clay's father and his uncle exchanged another glance. Then they both stared at Clay, their expressions expectant.

Clay couldn't think of a single appropriate thing to say right then, so he said nothing.

After a moment, his father prompted. "So then what else?"

"I don't know what you mean, Dad."

"I mean, did she tell you anything else?"

"Like what?"

Joe grunted, then muttered darkly, "Like who the hell the father is."

Ignoring the image of Jeff that flashed through his mind, Clay took a long drink from his beer, which he then set down very carefully upon a blue crocheted coaster atop the spindly-legged side table next to his chair. "No, she didn't tell me who the father is."

"It must be someone she really cares for," Joe insisted, looking rather piercingly at Clay. "We all know how she is. She's always been adventurous. But when it comes to men, she's choosy. She's just not the type for any one-night stand. She'd have to love the man first."

Clay had to force himself not to look away, out the picture window, where the snow was now coming down more steadily and the wind was starting to blow the white flakes into flurries.

His mind felt as if it was stuck. Stuck on Jeff.

And all of a sudden, it was starting to seem that there were only two possible ways to get *unstuck*. He could go to Andie again and demand she tell him who the father of her baby was. That might or might not get him an answer, depending on how stubborn Andie was going to end up being about this.

Or he could fly down to Brentwood for a little heart-to-heart talk with Jeff.

Of course, Jeff's new wife, Madeline, whom Clay really liked, would be there. Madeline had loved Jeff since the two of them were children. And now that Jeff was finally settling down and starting a life with her, Madeline was the happiest woman in the world.

"Don't you think so, Clay?" Joe was asking.

"Excuse me. Say that again?"

"I said, don't you think Andie would have to be in love before she would . . . become intimate with a man?"

Now what the hell was he going to say to that? Clay himself didn't believe in the kind of love his uncle was talking about. *Being in love,* as far as Clay was concerned, meant sexual attraction, plain and simple. It was nature's way of ensuring survival of the species and that was all. In Andie's case, he supposed, nature had done her job pretty well.

"Clay?" Joe was leaning forward, waiting for Clay to give some kind of answer.

"Yes," Clay said at last. "You're right. I'm sure Andie would have to really care for someone first. But honestly, I don't know who the man is. Andie told me she's going to have a baby and that she wants to stay on at Barrett and Company. That's all I know."

"Did she tell you she wants to raise the baby herself?" Joe's disapproval was painfully clear.

"Yes, she said that."

Joe shook his head. "I don't know how she'll manage. She's a good person, Andrea is. She means well. But where does she get her crazy ideas? The past few years, she's finally settled herself into a good job." He saluted Don with a quick nod. "Many thanks to you, Don—and you, too, Clay. Her mother and I are finally thinking we can relax— our Andie is all grown up now. And then, out of the blue, she comes to us and tells us she's going to be a mom— without a husband."

Clay sat up straighter in his chair, a strange emotion gripping him. It took him a moment to realize what he felt. It was defensiveness. For Andie, of all people.

"She's turned out to be damn good at her job," he heard himself saying. "Right, Dad?"

"Definitely," Don agreed without hesitation.

"I'm lucky to have her," Clay went on. Then he found himself paraphrasing Andie's words of the other night. "And since the father refuses to be a husband, then if Andie wants the baby, she has no choice. She has to raise it on her own."

Joe was sitting forward now. "She told you that? That the father didn't want her?"

Clay reached for his beer, found it empty and set it back on the coaster. "Uncle Joe, I respect you more than any man in the world, next to Dad, here. But these aren't questions to ask me. You should be asking Andie."

For a moment, Joe stared at him, a look so intense that Clay felt the short hairs rise on the back of his neck. Then Joe shot Don a speaking glance and Don took over again.

"Son, we've got to ask you..."

"What?"

"Is it you?"

Clay's mouth dropped open. He stared from one man to the other. "Me? The *father,* you mean?" He was baffled—and deeply hurt that his family could ever think he would betray their trust this way.

"God, Clay." Joe looked miserable. "Don't be insulted. We just felt we had to ask. It always seemed to us that there was...a little bit of an attraction between you and Andie."

"Attraction?" Clay repeated the word in total disbelief. "Between me and *Andie?* But we never could stand each other—you all knew that. You were always begging us not to fight, to try and get along with each other."

"Strong feelings are strong feelings," Joe said quietly. "Love and hate can be a lot alike."

Don added, "And since she works for you now, you two are thrown together every day. We couldn't help thinking that maybe you just got a little carried away."

"Not that you're the type to get carried away, Clay," Joe hastened to amend. "You've always been a down-to-earth young man and we all admire that in you."

"But what we're trying to say here," Don chimed in, "is if it did turn out to be you, well, that might not be such a terrible thing at all. You're not a blood relation to Andie, after all."

Clay felt the coiled tension inside him relax somewhat as he began to understand that they actually *wanted* him to be the one. For a moment, he had the most ridiculous urge to tell them they were right, the baby was his. He'd do the right thing and marry Andie immediately.

But the urge passed quickly, leaving him wondering what the hell his problem was. His cousin, the sworn enemy of his teenage years, was pregnant. And here he was, thinking about marrying her.

And did the family really think that the old animosity between Andie and him covered a mutual attraction? The idea was crazy. Totally crazy.

Clay held up his hands, palms out. "Sorry. It really isn't me."

Clay's father and his uncle seemed to sigh in unison. Clay thought they both looked older suddenly.

After a moment, Joe muttered, "Well, then. That's that, I suppose. But who the hell is it, then?"

Clay's father said, "I noticed she seemed awfully friendly with your buddy, Jeff, over the holidays."

Before Clay could think of what to say, Joe argued, "But I can't believe it could be him. He just got married, after all."

"That's right," Don agreed. "Clay flew down to be best man." He looked at Clay for confirmation.

"Yeah."

"And that was only a couple of weeks ago, wasn't it?"

"Right," Clay said, trying to sound normal and unconcerned, though his heart was galloping inside his chest. "Just a couple of weeks ago. On Valentine's Day."

In that stuck place in his mind, Clay saw Jeff and Madeline beneath an arbor that was covered in white roses, repeating their vows in clear, firm voices.

He also relived that moment when he'd gotten off the plane and Jeff had been there to meet him. Jeff had looked at him so strangely, he'd thought, a look both skeptical and anxious. But then Clay had reached out and grabbed Jeff in a bear hug. When they stepped away from each other and Jeff met Clay's eyes again, that strange look was gone.

"No, I'm sure it wasn't your friend," Joe said. "But I just don't know who else it could—"

"Listen, guys," Clay interrupted, thinking he couldn't take another moment of this. "I've told you everything I know. And, like I said before, it's Andie you should be talking to. I just plain don't like this, discussing her behind her back."

His uncle and his father regarded him solemnly.

At last his father conceded, "All right, Clay. If that's how you feel."

Clay stayed for dinner, though it was a rather strained affair. His mother kept looking at him hopefully. But he knew she wouldn't ask him any uncomfortable questions. She would be tactful and wait until she had her husband alone to find out what had transpired between the men. He made it easy on her and left early so she could quiz his father in private.

The storm that had started with a few moist snowflakes drifting quietly down had steadily worsened. By the time Clay left his parents' house, the winds were up and the snow was coming down thick and heavy. The roads were a mess, so it took him nearly an hour to travel the fifteen miles to his two-story house on ten acres out at the end of twisting Wildriver Road.

Once there, he mixed himself a whiskey and soda and went out on the top deck outside his bedroom to watch the black storm clouds rise and roll in the night sky. His house was at a lower elevation than his parents' place in town, so he was pelted with freezing rain rather than snow. Within two minutes, he was drenched to the skin.

But he didn't give a damn. Clay loved storms. He was a very orderly, controlled man, as a rule. But even as a young child he'd always stepped out to feel the rain on his face when he could, to watch thunderheads gather and lightning fork across the sky.

He loved the wildness of a storm. It soothed something inside him.

His biological mother had loved storms. Somewhere, way back in the farthest reaches of his early memories, he could still see her, wearing a cheap red coat, arms outstretched, head tipped up to the sky. She was spinning in circles, laughing, in the middle of a lawn in front of a building where they had a small apartment. The rain poured down on her face and the wind whipped at her flimsy coat.

She didn't care. She laughed and laughed. "Isn't it fabulous, Clay, baby? Can't you feel it, just moving all through you? Oh, I do love a storm. A storm is just grand!"

Clay lifted his whiskey and soda and saluted the black, heavy sky. Then he took a bracing drink, leaving his head tipped up when he was finished, so the icy rain could sting his cheeks. He watched as a claw of lightning ripped the center out of the night. Thunder roared and seemed to roll off down the hills toward the distant valleys.

Maybe that was the one thing Rita Cox had left to him, he thought as he at last lowered his head. Her legacy to him had been the peace he could find in the untamed heart of a big storm.

She certainly hadn't left him much else. She bore him out of wedlock. The line for *father* on his birth certificate was taken up with one word: *unknown*. If Rita knew whose name should have gone there, she'd never told him.

She'd been a woman who could barely take care of herself, was often ill, moving from job to job. She hadn't been equipped to take care of a little boy. Yet she would never give him up. So sometimes he lived with her and sometimes, when times were bad, he lived in foster care or at a home for dependent children. When he was nine, she'd died of a ruptured appendix.

Her death, he understood later, was his big chance. He was free, then, to be adopted. To find the Barretts. To have a real family at last.

He wondered, standing there, soaked and shivering, holding an empty drink, if he was finally zeroing in on the truth about this whole mess with Andie. If he was finally seeing what bothered him so damn much when he thought about Andie and the baby she insisted she was going to raise alone.

His own memories were the problem. His memories of a mother who wouldn't give him up and yet couldn't take care of him, either.

Clay knew in the logical part of his brain that Andie and Rita were not the same at all. Andie was strong and healthy. She had a steady job that she could and would hold on to. She had a devoted family who, once they accepted that she was determined to raise her child alone, would give her all the love and support in the world.

And yet one aspect of the situation would be exactly the same as it had been for Rita. On Andie's baby's birth certificate, the father's name would be *unknown*.

Clay lifted his head to the streaming sky again. The rain beat on his face. He waited to feel set free, lifted outside himself.

The release didn't come. Somehow, tonight, the storm was bringing him no peace at all.

He tossed his ice cubes over the railing and went back inside to mix himself another stiff one.

The next morning, the sun came out. The world was bathed in that cold, thin brightness that often follows a winter storm.

Clay rose early and showered away the fuzziness from one too many whiskey and sodas. Sometime deep in the night, he had come to accept what he had to do.

He called an airline that scheduled a lot of flights between Sacramento and L.A. Luck was with him. He gave his credit card number and paid for a seat on an 11:00 a.m. flight.

He threw a few things in an overnight bag and headed for the Sacramento airport. He would arrive in L.A. at a little after noon. And not too long after that, he would be knocking on Jeff Kirkland's door.

Chapter Four

Clay had a little trouble finding Jeff and Madeline's house in Brentwood. He had never been there before. The house had been a wedding present from Madeline's father, who ran a real estate business.

But at last, with the help of a *Thomas's Guide* he bought at a convenience store, Clay drove his rental car onto the right street and parked in front of an attractive Spanish-style house with a big magnolia tree in the middle of its graciously sloping front lawn.

Clay knew he couldn't afford to hesitate, or he just might turn the car around and head back the way he'd come. The moment he turned off the engine, he got out of the car and strode up the curving brick walk that led to the front door.

The door had a little window on top, with miniature wrought-iron bars over it. A few moments after Clay rang the bell, a woman's face appeared behind the bars. Clay didn't recognize her.

"Yes?" Her voice crackled from the little speaker to the right of the door.

"Is this the Kirkland residence?"

"Yes."

Clay realized this must be a housekeeper or a maid. "I'd like to speak with Jeff—or Madeline. I'm Clay. Clay Barrett."

"Just a minute. You wait, please."

The woman disappeared. Clay waited, calculating the days since the wedding. He wondered if Jeff and Madeline were still in the Bahamas.

He was just beginning to believe he'd flown all the way to L.A. for nothing when he saw Madeline's face through the little barred window.

Her gray eyes lit up. "Clay!" He heard her disengage the locks and then she threw back the door and grabbed him in a hug. "What a surprise!" Her delighted laughter chimed in his ear. "This is great. Just terrific."

She straightened her arms and held him away from her. "Jeff's upstairs. Come on in." She pulled him through a small foyer into a big room with a fireplace and glass doors that led out to a shaded patio. Couches, tables and bookcases were stacked every which way and there were packing boxes everywhere.

"Don't mind the mess," she instructed. "We just got back. It was heaven. Heaven, I'm telling you. But now it's move-in time. From heaven straight to hell." She cast a glance at the ceiling and put a hand to the side of her face, as if she was afraid her head might roll off. Then she laughed again.

Clay looked at her, slim and pretty in jeans and a simple cotton shirt. Happiness shone from her, turned her prettiness very close to beauty. He'd known her almost as long as he'd known Jeff, since that first year of college, when Jeff had taken Clay to a party at one of the huge, estate-like houses in the neighborhood where Jeff had grown up. Madeline had been at that party, bright and friendly and so in love with Jeff that it was almost painful to see.

Clay learned soon enough what the story was. Madeline's and Jeff's mothers were best friends. Their fathers were partners in a successful real estate business. As babies, Madeline and Jeff had shared the same playpen. They'd played together as kids and gone steady in high school. All Madeline wanted was to be with Jeff. But Jeff said he had some serious living to do before he was going to be ready to even think about settling down.

Three years ago, both Jeff's parents had died of different illnesses just a few months apart. Madeline had comforted him. They'd moved in together. Jeff had taken his rightful place in the real estate firm.

Jeff and Madeline had finally become engaged a few months before Clay moved back to northern California. The wedding had been planned for New Year's Eve.

And a week before Christmas, Jeff had shown up on Clay's doorstep.

"Hey, bud. Can you spare me a bed for a week or two? I need a little space."

Clay had known instantly what was going on. His best friend was suffering from a serious case of cold feet. "What about the wedding?"

Jeff shook his head. "There isn't going to be one. I called it off."

Clay tried not to be judgmental. Being judgmental with Jeff never did any good, anyway. But he couldn't help pointing out, "You're making a big mistake, my friend. Madeline's the best thing that ever happened to you."

Jeff's square jaw hardened. "Can I stay or not?"

Clay had stepped back to let him in.

"Clay? Yoo-hoo, anybody in there?" Madeline's wide smile was wobbling a little.

Clay blinked. "Oh. Sorry. Just thinking."

"Is this something serious, then?" The smile had faded completely now, to be replaced by an uneasy frown.

"What?"

"The reason you're here."

"No," he baldly lied. "Not at all. Not serious at all. I was... I had to see an old client in Century City. Tax time coming up, you know?"

"Oh. I see." It was obvious she didn't.

"I just thought I'd drop in, on the off chance you two might be around."

She smiled again. "Well. I'm glad you did."

"Yeah." It was Jeff's voice. "Always glad to see a friend."

Clay looked up. Jeff was leaning against an arch that led to a hallway. He wore the bottom half of a pair of cotton pajamas and his muscular arms were crossed over his bare chest. His pose was relaxed. But Clay didn't miss the watchfulness in his eyes.

"There you are, lazybones." Madeline wrinkled her nose at him. "Clay's here."

"I can see that."

Clay remembered his objective. He had to get Jeff alone. "Had lunch yet?"

Madeline chuckled. "Oh, please. He hasn't had *breakfast* yet. As a matter of fact, I was just going to see if I could find some eggs and a frying pan in my disaster of a kitchen. Any takers?"

Both Clay and Jeff were silent, looking at each other.

Madeline glanced from one to the other and back again. "Hey, I swear it won't take long. I'll get Marina to help me."

Jeff shrugged. "Naw. Let's go out." His voice was off-hand. His eyes were not. He looked down at his pajama bottoms and the bare feet sticking out of them. "I'll get decent."

Clay valiantly cast about for a way to convince Madeline to stay behind without making her suspicious about this visit all over again.

Madeline did it for him. "Listen. I adore you both and there's nothing I'd like better than a long, leisurely lunch with the two of you. But look at this place. I've got to get going on it." She gave Clay a soulful look. "Please understand."

Clay tried to look regretful, though what he actually felt was relief. "All right. I'll forgive you. Just this once."

Ten minutes later, Clay and Jeff sat in Clay's rental car. Jeff suggested a place he knew out in Santa Monica. Clay drove in silence, dealing with the traffic and trying to think how he was going to phrase what he had to say.

When they were almost to the restaurant, Jeff spoke up. "I'm not really hungry."

Clay glanced at his friend. "Me, neither."

"Let's go to the beach."

They went on to where the highway met the ocean. Clay found a parking space easily. They walked down to the beach, where the winter wind had a bite to it in spite of the cloudless sky. Overhead, the gulls soared. A few hardy surfers and boogie-boarders tackled some rather puny waves.

Clay and Jeff sat down side by side, wrapped their arms loosely around their drawn-up knees and stared out at the waves.

Jeff said, "I was wondering when you'd show up." His voice was flat, matter-of-fact.

Clay's throat felt tight. "You were?"

Jeff shot Clay a look, then grunted. "Come on. You were bound to figure it out." Jeff gave a humorless laugh.

"I told your cousin that. But she still held on to her hopeless idea that you wouldn't have to know."

Clay found he couldn't speak for a moment. Then he asked, "It's true, then?"

Jeff looked down at the sand between his knees. "Yeah."

Clay stared hard at the ocean as the truth came to him. It hurt. Bad. But just knowing wasn't enough. The words had been too vague. It had to be said bluntly so there would never be any doubt concerning it.

Clay said, "You had sex with my cousin."

Beside him, Jeff didn't move. "Yeah."

"Why?"

"Hell. Why? How do I know why? Because it was New Year's Eve, the night I should have married Madeline. And I'd called Madeline. And she wouldn't speak to me. Because I was confused and hurting and wanted to forget it all. Because your cousin was *there*, sweet and pretty and soft. We had too much champagne. And it happened. I know it's hard for someone like you to understand, since control is more or less your middle name. But sometimes, for ordinary guys with weaknesses, things just get out of hand."

"Things get out of hand." Clay repeated Jeff's words with great precision.

"Yes."

For a moment, Clay said nothing. Then he swore low and feelingly. "You're dead right about one thing. I don't understand. You didn't even think to use a condom, did you?"

"No. I didn't. I was a jackass. Believe me. I realize that."

"You were my friend. Staying in my house."

"I know."

"You spent the night with my cousin—because she was *there*, and then you came back here to L.A. and you patched things up with Madeline. You *married* Madeline, even though Andie had called you and told you she was going to have a baby. I was at your wedding. I was your best man. And you never said a damn word."

"Guilty. On all counts."

Clay couldn't bear to look at Jeff, couldn't seem to get his mind around the enormity of Jeff's betrayal. He wanted to hurt Jeff right then. He wanted to do him great bodily harm. At the same time, scenes from their ten-year friendship kept playing in his head.

Though Jeff was silent beside him, it seemed to Clay that he could hear his friend's reckless laughter as Jeff burst into Clay's room at the dorm back in college and dragged him off to a beach party or an impromptu baseball game somewhere.

More than once, Jeff had shaken Clay awake at midnight, demanding he throw on some clothes and go with him to a cantina on Alvarado Street, where there was this little *señorita* who could play eight ball like no one you ever saw. Or he'd haul Clay over to some loft downtown, where he'd introduce him to a punk poet with spiked pink hair. They'd stay up all night, the poet reciting, Clay and Jeff listening, talking, laughing. Having fun.

And later, after college was over, when Clay was killing himself to learn the ropes on the audit staff of Stanley, Beeson and Means, Jeff would climb in the window of Clay's apartment with a six-pack under one arm and five Clint Eastwood videos under the other. He'd refuse to go away until Clay drank half of the beer and watched, at the very least, *A Fistful of Dollars*.

Clay had come to L.A. to prove himself, to learn his trade from the best of the best. He had always intended to return home eventually and put what he'd learned to work in the business he would inherit from his father. But the long years of schooling and apprenticeship had been hard for him. He missed the mountains, missed his family.

Jeff, almost singlehandedly, had made life in L.A. bearable for Clay. Having a friend like Jeff made the drudgery endurable. Life in L.A. was okay.

Jeff was like Andie, Clay realized. Jeff was laughter and adventure and a hell of a lot of fun. But with Andie, Clay had always been outside looking in. With Jeff, it was different. There was no family rivalry with Jeff. There were only good feelings and good times.

And now Jeff had done this. The unforgivable. And the unforgivable had produced new life.

Clay pointed out carefully, ''Andie says the baby won't have your name.''

Jeff let out a low groan. ''Look. Your cousin wants to raise the baby alone. She doesn't *want* me to help her. And things are good now, with me and Madeline. I just don't want to mess that up. Can't you understand?''

''You're saying you don't want Madeline to know.''

''Right. It would break her heart.''

''You'd deny your own child, just so Madeline wouldn't have to know?''

''Your cousin doesn't want it to be my child.''

''That's a feeble excuse. You know it. It *is* your child, no matter what Andie says.''

''If she's willing to take full responsibility, then she and I are agreed. It's the way it will be.''

''She might change her mind. Women have been known to do that.''

''I'll deal with that if and when it happens.''

Clay thought of Andie, of the proud set to her chin and the absolute determination in her eyes when she'd said, *''The man is out of my—our—lives. For good and all.''*

"You know it's not going to happen, don't you?" Clay taunted. "You'll never have to deal with it. Another woman might change her mind, but not Andie. She's too proud. So you're deserting her *and* your baby, that's what you're doing."

"It's how she wants it."

"That doesn't matter. You're turning your back on your responsibility. You're just walking away."

Jeff grabbed a tiny shell from the sand and tossed it overhand, out toward the waves. Then turned his head and met Clay's eyes. "You set such damn impossible standards. For yourself and everyone else. Well, I can't live up to those standards. That's all there is to it. What the hell else do you want from me?"

"Nothing," Clay said flatly, realizing it was true at the same time as he said it. "I want you out of my life. And my cousin's life. I never want to see or hear from you again. As far as I'm concerned, you're dead."

Clay watched the emotions chase themselves across Jeff's face. Pain. Anger. Sadness. Relief.

Clay turned the knife. "Look. If you don't want Madeline to know, it's the best way."

"I know that, damn you." Jeff stood. He held a hand down to Clay.

Clay stared up at him, not moving. "Well?"

Jeff stuck his hand in his pocket. Overhead, the gulls wheeled. One cried out, a long, lonely sound.

"All right, bud." A faraway smile curved Jeff's mouth. "I'm dead."

Clay got to his feet unaided. The two men stood, one brown haired, one blond, both tall and well built, facing each other on the sand.

Jeff's distant smile turned knowing. "You ain't really all *that* civilized, are you now, bud?"

Clay shrugged, though the violence within him seemed to make the air shimmer in front of his eyes.

"I'll make it easy for you," Jeff said. Then his fist shot out and connected with Clay's jaw.

Chapter Five

There was a moment of stark pain, then an explosion behind Clay's eyes. Clay staggered back.

And then, at last, he was set free to act. His body broke the reins of his iron control.

With a guttural cry, Clay sent his own fist flying. Flesh and cartilage gave way. Jeff grunted in pain.

Clay kicked him before Jeff could recover. Jeff stumbled back. Clay jumped on him and brought him down.

The two men rolled, struggling, over and over in the sand. Above, the gulls cried and soared. The waves tumbled in and slid away again, on and on, without end.

Eventually, when pain and exhaustion finally conquered them both, the two men dragged themselves to their feet and reeled back to Clay's rental car.

Clay drove Jeff to Brentwood and dropped him off under the wide canopy of the magnolia tree in front of the

gracefully sloping lawn. Then he went to the airport to wait
for a return flight.

It was well after midnight when he finally fell into his
bed.

"Good Lord, Clay," Andie demanded when he walked
into the office the next morning, "what *happened?*"

He gingerly touched the purple bruise on the side of his
jaw. "What, this?"

"Yes. And that and that." She indicated his black eye
and the cut on the bridge of his nose.

"I fell off my tractor." Clay owned a miniature tractor
the size of a riding mower that he used to move dirt and tree
stumps around on his ten acres of land.

Andie wasn't convinced. "Fell off your tractor, right.
You'll lose your Eagle Scout badge telling lies like that.
Now what is going on?"

Clay lied some more. "Nothing." He had already decided she was never going to know the truth about this. "I
went out for a drink last night and I chose the wrong bar,
that's all."

"That's not like you, Clay."

"What? Going out for a drink or going to the wrong
bar?"

"Neither. It's something else. What?"

"God, you're nosy." He peered at her more closely. "But
you're looking good. Really good." It was true. The shadows beneath her eyes were gone and there was color in her
cheeks again.

"You're not going to tell me what happened, are you?"

"No, I'm not. As I said, it's nothing. And you *are* looking good."

She was quiet for a moment. He knew she was making up
her mind whether to keep after him about the source of his
injuries. He was relieved when she gave a small shrug and

admitted, "I'm feeling much better. Since we talked last week, a lot of what was worrying me isn't worrying me anymore. It's amazing what a few good nights of sleep will do."

"Well, great." He realized he should probably get his coffee and move along to his own office down the hall. But he didn't move.

While he leaned on the reception counter and grinned at her, Andie mentioned that one of the bigger accounts he'd inherited from his father had left a message on the service. "He said he's dropping in this morning some time."

"Nice of him to let us know."

"I pulled his file. It's on your desk."

"You are incredibly efficient."

"Maybe I should get a raise."

"Maybe I should get to work."

She laughed. "Fine. Get to work. But I'm not giving up about that raise. And Clay..."

"What?"

"Are you sure you're all right?"

"I'm fine. Really. Though I've got to admit I'm kind of dreading facing Mrs. Faulkenberry looking like this." Mrs. Faulkenberry had been coming to Barrett & Co. to have her tax return prepared for as long as Clay could remember. Every year, she brought in her receipts in a shoe box and handed them over to Clay's father personally. This year, she'd agreed to hand over the precious shoe box to Clay. She was due in at one that afternoon.

"Don't worry about Mrs. Faulkenberry," Andie reassured him. "She's seen worse things in her time than a beat up accountant, I'm sure."

"I'll take that under advisement."

"Good." She swiveled in her chair and faced her computer screen again.

Clay looked at her delicate profile for a moment before he finally went to pour himself some coffee and get to work.

When Clay arrived home that night, there was a message on his answering machine from Jill Peters, a woman he'd dated a few times last fall and during the holidays. In fact, Jill had been his date on New Year's Eve, the night Jeff and Andie had—

Clay cut the thought off before it was finished and forced himself to keep his mind on Jill. Jill had tickets to a Kings game for Friday night and wanted Clay to go with her.

Clay played the message twice, thinking that he'd enjoyed being with Jill and realizing that more than two months had slipped by since the last time he'd talked to her. He probably should have called her.

But he hadn't. And now he knew that he was going to get back to her and tell her he appreciated her invitation, but it was no go.

He didn't know why, exactly.

He called her quickly and made his excuses and then wondered for a moment or two what was the matter with him, to turn down a pleasant evening with a nice woman.

But then he shrugged and forgot about it. There was no sense in dwelling on it. It was just one of those things.

He thought of Andie right then, for some reason, and realized he was looking forward to going to work tomorrow. The confrontation with Jeff was behind him and Andie was feeling better. Things should be more pleasant at the office from now on.

And they were. All that week, things went smoothly.

Andie told him in a private moment that she knew her father and his father had ganged up on him.

"But you were steadfast, as always," she jokingly praised him. "You didn't give out or give in."

He actually put on a wise-guy voice. "I told you I was no snitch." He was careful to add offhandedly, "Not that there was anything I could have told them. I mean, what do I know, anyway?"

She gave him an odd, pensive look. "That's right. What do you know, anyway?"

Something tightened down inside him. He felt a twinge of guilt. But what was the point of telling the truth here? Jeff was out of her life and Clay's life, as well. Dragging it all out now would only cause her more pain than she'd already suffered.

One of her sleek eyebrows lifted slightly. "Something *is* bothering you. Isn't it, Clay?"

But then the door buzzer rang, telling them there was someone out front.

"Better see who it is," he said softly.

She gave a little sigh and left.

The subject did not present itself again—not immediately, anyway. And that was fine with Clay.

The work load seemed to get heavier every day. They were managing fine, but there wasn't a lot of time for anything but the job. As the first week of March faded into the second, they fell into the habit of ordering take-out food and eating dinner together right there at the office after the last appointment of the day. Then Andie would get to work on the day's time sheets, while Clay would dig into the next tax summary. They'd say good-night at eight or so and start all over again twelve hours later.

Andie said she didn't mind the long hours at all. She was feeling better every day, and she did need the extra money.

Clay believed she really was feeling better. Her eyes were clear and bright now, and though the soda crackers were still ready at her desk, her appetite had definitely improved. Some evenings, he had to watch out or she was likely to eat half of *his* dinner as well as her own.

It was Wednesday night in the second week of March when Clay's mother called him at home.

"Clay, dear, Saturday is Andie's birthday. Did you remember?"

"Yes, Mom."

Clay *had* remembered. He'd been planning to use the event as an excuse to take Andie out to dinner and present her with a nice big check that would be part bonus and part birthday gift.

But the family, evidently, had plans of their own. "We thought we'd have a little party. Just the family and a few close friends."

"I see."

"You sound guarded, dear."

"I'm not. The truth is, I already had something planned for Andie's birthday, that's all."

"You did?" His mother's voice was suddenly bright.

"It wasn't anything important. I was going to take her out to dinner."

"Why, I think that sounds lovely. Maybe you could do both."

"What do you mean, both?"

"Come to the party *and* buy her a nice meal."

"I'll think about it. Tell me about the party."

His mother launched into the plans. It was to be at Thelma and Joe's on Saturday afternoon. "You will come, won't you, Clay?"

Clay promised to attend.

"And don't tell Andie. It's supposed to be a surprise."

"I won't say a word."

"Good. Come at one-thirty, no later. We want everyone there to yell 'Surprise!' when she walks in."

"I'll be there."

His mother rambled on again, about how Andie's best friend, Ruth Ann Pardo, was going to go to Andie's apartment early Saturday morning, to make sure Andie didn't go anywhere. Then Aunt Thelma was going to call Andie at the right time with a trumped-up emergency and beg her to come right over.

"I think it should work, don't you, Clay?"

"Sure, Mom."

"Oh, and do get her something extra nice. She needs all our love and affection right now." His mother's tone was heavy with meaning.

Clay smiled to himself. Slowly, as Clay had known they would, the family was coming to grips with the reality of Andie's pregnancy. Everyone was still speaking in low tones and oblique phrases about it. But that would pass. By the time the baby actually made his or her appearance, they'd all be lined up at the observation window in the hospital nursery, jockeying for their first glimpse of the newest member of the clan.

He promised his mother he'd get Andie something nice and then he said goodbye.

Clay ended up doing as his mother suggested. He planned to attend the party and he also took Andie to dinner on Friday night and gave her the bonus check.

Her eyes misted over a little when she looked at the amount. "I should tell you it's too much."

"But you won't." He raised his wineglass and toasted her with it. "Because you know it's not only a birthday present."

"It isn't?"

"Hell, no. It's also a bonus check."

"Ah. For the terrific job I'm doing at the office."

"Exactly."

"Then you're right. It's not too much. I'm worth every cent."

Andie ate all of her salmon and had chocolate mousse for dessert. Clay watched her with satisfaction, thinking that she was doing a pretty good job of eating for two.

When they left the restaurant, which was on one of the two major streets in downtown Meadow Valley, a light snow was falling. Andie put out her hands to catch a few flakes. The bracelet of linked hearts that she always wore gleamed on her wrist as it caught the light of the street-lamp beside her. "Snow. In March."

"It happens. Sometimes as late as April."

"Yes." Her smile was so womanly—knowing, and yet shy. "But spring is near. I can feel it." She flipped up the collar of her winter coat. "Come on. Let's go."

Clay flipped up his collar to match hers and they set off up the sidewalk. When they reached the corner, they instinctively moved closer together against the chill of the wind that swept between the buildings. Since the restaurant's small lot in back was full, they'd both parked on the street.

"I'll walk you to your car," Clay suggested.

Andie sent him a smile that seemed to warm the icy air between them. "Thanks."

Andie's car, a little red compact that had seen better days, was waiting two blocks away. When they reached it, she turned to him.

"Thanks, Clay. It was lovely."

"You're welcome." He stared down at her.

The snow caught on her eyelashes and sparkled like tiny diamonds in her nearly black hair. She always pulled her hair back for work, so it looked like a sleek cap on her head. But it had a lot of curl to it and the moisture in the air was working on it. Little tendrils were curling now around her face.

It occurred to Clay, in a dazed sort of way, that something was happening here.

"Can I drive you to your car?" she offered.

"No. It's okay. The walk will do me good."

"You're sure?"

"Absolutely."

She rose on tiptoe. Her lips brushed his cheek, right above the pale remnant of the bruise where Jeff's first punch had landed.

Clay felt the warmth of her breath, smelled the fresh sweetness of her skin. Inside his trousers, his manhood stirred. The pleasant ache shocked him for an instant.

And then something deep inside him gave way. And it was okay. He could allow himself to desire her.

"Good night, then," she said.

"Yes. Good night."

She ran around to the driver's side, unlocked the door and got in. The car started up with a grumbling whine. She pulled out and drove away. Clay watched her go. She'd disappeared around a corner before he shook himself and started for his own car.

The next day at two o'clock, Clay jumped out from behind his Aunt Thelma's couch and hollered "Surprise!" at the top of his lungs. The only thing that kept him from feeling like a complete idiot when he did it was that everyone else around him was doing the same thing.

If Andie wasn't surprised, she did a good job of acting the part. She jumped backward, put her hand to her throat and squealed, "Omigod!"

And then everyone was laughing and hugging her and shouting, "Happy Birthday!"

Clay stood back from all the commotion a little, watching Andie smile and laugh, seeing how she charmed everyone. And feeling thoroughly charmed himself. "She's a captivator, our Andie is," his great-uncle Jerry whispered slyly in his ear.

Clay gave the old man a smile. "Yes. She is."

Uncle Jerry ran his liver-spotted hand over the crown of his head, as if smoothing his hair back, even though he was totally bald. "If I were thirty years younger..."

"You'd still be married to Aunt Bette," Clay reminded him.

Uncle Jerry guffawed. "Damned if you ain't right, my boy. Damned if you ain't right. And where is that wife of mine, anyway?"

Clay pointed to a chair by the wall, where Great-aunt Bette was sitting with another of the great-aunts. Uncle Jerry tottled off in their direction.

"She *is* looking better, don't you think, dear?" Clay's mother, who'd appeared at his side out of nowhere, asked him in a hushed tone.

Clay nodded.

"Did you get her something nice?"

"Mother."

"What?" Della's eyes widened in an expression much too innocent for a woman who was almost sixty years of age. "What did I do?"

Clay just looked at her, a look of great patience.

"Well, I was just checking."

"I gave her a huge bonus."

His mother beamed. "That's wonderful. She can use that." But then she frowned. "But it's not very personal."

"Mother," Clay said again.

"Oh, all right. All right. I'm minding my own business. Starting now."

"That's good news."

"But Andie *is* looking lovely..."

"Yes, she is."

"And I...oh, never mind." She shook her head distractedly and wandered away to talk to her own mother, Granny Sid Santangelo, who was sitting on the couch, holding forth to anyone who would listen about how things used to be and ought to be again.

For the next couple of hours, Clay wandered from room to room, listening to the conversations, answering his relatives when they asked him questions and following Andie with his eyes.

She was so many things to him. His cousin. The passionate rival of his youth. His crackerjack, indispensable office manager.

And now there was more.

He'd always known she captivated people. People called her appealing and engaging and fun. He'd seen the way she charmed everyone, so they let her get away with things that Clay would never have been allowed to do. He'd resented her for her ability to enchant—at the same time as he'd called himself immune.

But now, he realized as he watched her opening her presents, oohing and aahing over each and every one, he *wasn't* immune. He wasn't quite sure how it had happened—something about the baby probably, and all the buried pain and memories the baby's existence had stirred up.

Whatever. The point was, it *had* happened. It was as if he had spent twenty years keeping an invisible wall between himself and the awareness that she was someone he could desire. And then, last night on a side street in his hometown, he'd suddenly discovered that the wall was gone. He didn't even know exactly when he'd let it crumble. But it wasn't there now.

The facts ran through his mind.

There was no blood tie between them. They were a great team at the office. If they married, the family would be thrilled and the baby would have a father.

Hell, for the baby's sake alone, it was certainly something to consider.

"Deep in thought as usual," a rough voice behind him remarked.

Clay turned, already smiling. "Johnny." Johnny Pardo still wore his hair too long and preferred black leather jackets and battered jeans to respectable clothing, but other than that he was all grown up now. Ten years ago, he'd shocked everyone at Meadow Valley High by marrying Andie's best friend, Ruth Ann Pagneti. Everyone had said that the marriage would never last, that Ruth Ann was a smart-mouthed, sheltered schoolgirl who knew nothing about real life, while Johnny was surly and troubled and would never settle down.

A decade later, they were still going strong. They had two boys. Johnny owned and ran a franchise convenience store and coached little league in his spare time.

"I gotta have a smoke," Johnny growled.

"I thought you quit."

"I did. I quit more than any guy I ever met. Come outside with me. If Ruth Ann sees me, I'm gonna get the look."

"What look?"

"The how-can-you-hurt-yourself-this-way-you're-hurting-all-of-us-who-love-you-too look. I can't take that. I just want a puff or two."

Clay went out in the chilly backyard with Johnny. He watched as Johnny lit up, and tried not to smile at the absurdly ecstatic smile on the other man's face as the hazardous fumes filled his lungs.

"We are talkin' nirvana, man," Johnny remarked. "So what were you thinkin' about in there?"

"Hell. Life."

"That deep, huh?"

"Yeah, I guess."

"Your cousin looks good."

"So everyone keeps telling me."

"You don't think so?"

"No. I think so. I think she looks great."

Johnny blew out smoke through his nose and then chuckled. "Remember that time I took her riding on my motorcycle and you got all hot and bothered about it?"

"I remember."

"I always thought you had a thing for her."

"No kidding?"

"No kidding." Johnny dropped his cigarette to the grass, stepped on it and then carefully stowed the smashed butt in his jacket pocket. Then he launched into one of his favorite subjects: the Bulls and the Suns. A few minutes later, Ruth Ann appeared.

"There you two are. I've been looking all over." She marched up to her husband and put her arm through his. "P.U. Cigarettes."

"Gimme a kiss."

Ruth Ann groaned, but she did lift her mouth. Her husband lightly pecked her lips. She turned to Clay, her dark eyes dancing, her pointed chin high. "He adores me."

"I can see."

"Come on inside now. Both of you. Andie's going to cut the cake."

There were twenty-eight candles on the chocolate fudge cake that Aunt Thelma had baked. Andie's hair was loose, in a dark cloud around her face. She had to gather it up in a fist, and hold it at her neck so it would be safe from the lit candles.

Aunt Thelma urged, "Hurry up, they're melting."

Andie's face glowed as she bent over the yellow flames. She closed her eyes.

"Andie..."

"Shh, quiet, Mom. Let me make my wish."

A hush fell over the room. Clay watched Andie's wish take form as a slow, secret smile made her glowing face shine brighter still.

"There," she said, with quiet satisfaction, her eyes still shut. "I see it. Just the way I want it to be."

"Then hurry..."

"All right, all right." She opened her eyes and sucked in a huge breath. And damned if she didn't get every last candle at one try.

Everyone applauded and Andie cut the cake.

Clay took his piece and sat in the living room near enough to Granny Sid that he had to listen to a long diatribe about the youth of today and how there was very little hope for them. When he'd finished his cake, he got up and solemnly told her that she was absolutely right—things were not what they had once been.

Then he kissed her wrinkled cheek. "See you later, Granny Sid."

Her little black eyes impaled him. "You're a smart boy, Clay."

"Thank you, Granny."

"Maybe too smart for your own good."

"Now what's *that* supposed to mean, Granny?"

"Stop thinking so much," Granny advised. "Give your heart a chance to talk."

He chucked her under her wattled chin. "What would a heart say, Granny, if it could talk?"

Granny cackled. "See there, see what I mean? You don't even believe that a heart can talk, now do you?"

He considered teasing her some more, but decided to answer honestly. "No, Granny. I'm afraid I don't."

She shook her head. "Then what more can I say? We're talking different languages. But that's all right. You just go on. I know you're in a rush. Young people. Always in a rush." She patted him on the arm, dismissing him as if he were still ten years old and waiting for her permission to go outside and play.

He found his aunt Thelma before he left.

"Great cake, Aunt Thelma."

"Have another piece."

"No, I've got to go."

"What's your hurry?" Andie was suddenly beside him, grinning up at him, her midnight hair a halo around her face, the scent of her like roses and peaches combined. How could he have known her all these years and never noticed the enticing, wonderful way that she smelled?

"I've really got to go." He cringed at the lame sound of his own voice.

Andie leaned closer and whispered in his ear, "You'll be sorry. Aunt Bette's going to be getting out her ukulele any minute now."

The same thing that had happened on the street last night occurred again. He felt himself growing hard. It took all the will he possessed not to turn his head and capture her mouth.

Somehow, he managed to remember himself enough to back away from her a little and give a low groan. "That settles it. I'm outta here."

Thelma patted his shoulder and reached up to kiss his cheek. "Thanks for coming, Clay."

"I enjoyed it." He turned to Andie. "Walk me to my car?"

She blinked and her soft lips parted in mild surprise. The request had been just a fraction out of the ordinary. He was only one guest of many, and she saw him nearly every day.

"Oh, go on with him, honey," Aunt Thelma said.

"All right." Andie's face was composed again. She smiled and hooked her arm through his. "Let's go."

Clay felt the warmth of her against his side. It was good, he decided. It was *right*. It was as it should be.

They walked down to the foot of the street, where Clay's car waited. Whatever snow had clung to the ground from the night before was gone now, melted away to nothing by the afternoon sun. Andie held on to his arm, her step in time with his.

He wondered what the hell to do.

He could kiss her. He could stop right there on the sidewalk and turn her to him. He could pull her soft body close and lift her chin with his hand.

Or maybe he should say something, something that would let her know what he was feeling, something that would communicate to her in just a few words everything that was going through his mind.

They reached the car too soon. He still hadn't figured out quite what to do, or what to say.

He turned and leaned against the passenger door. "Andie, I..."

"What?"

"Well, I..."

"Yes?" She folded her arms over her breasts and shivered a little. But she was wearing a huge, soft sweater and leggings and the sun was out. If she trembled, it wasn't from cold.

"There's something I..."

"What?" She bit the inside of her lip. Her nostrils flared, just slightly. He thought of a soft, vulnerable animal scenting a predator.

"Hell." He only breathed the word.

"What? Clay, what is it?"

He had no words. He wanted to touch her. He dared to reach out and cup his hand over her upper arm. Her sweater was as soft as it looked. Beneath that softness, she was firm and warm. Her arm tensed under his fingers.

"Clay, what?" She backed away, out from under his touch.

"Andie..."

Clay couldn't help himself. He reached out and took her arm in a firmer grip. She stared at him, stunned. He pulled her to him.

She came, falling against him with a tiny exhalation of breath. He felt the soft fullness of her breasts against his chest.

"Clay, what is it?" She lifted her head to search his eyes. "What do you want?"

He said it. "You."

He watched her face, watched for the signs. There would be nothing, of course, if she gave him no sign. But the signs *were* there. She didn't—or couldn't—hide them. There was that little hitch of breath, the quickened heartbeat against his own. And most important, he saw the way her dark eyes went cloudy and her lips grew suddenly soft. He took the signs into himself, hoarding them.

It was okay. She hadn't rejected him.

Very slowly and deliberately he lowered his mouth and tasted her, as he'd wanted to do back there in the house.

She sighed. He felt that sigh all through him, felt her body giving, pressed to his. He thought of roses and peaches again, thought that she tasted just the way she smelled. Her mouth, softly parted, allowed the questing entrance of his tongue.

It was silky and hot inside her mouth. So good, and so exactly what he'd imagined it might be. Yes, he did want her. Badly. He swept the sweet, moist inner flesh of her mouth with his tongue.

She moaned, low and hungrily.

And then she stiffened.

"No." Andie breathed the word against his lips.

She gripped him by the arms and pushed herself away from him.

Clay wanted to grab her and pull her back, to take her mouth again, to savor the taste of her just a little bit more. Desire was an ache in him. But he controlled it. He was good at controlling himself, after all. And he'd found out what he needed to know.

There was a long, gaping moment of silence between them. A bird squawked at them from a wire overhead. On the street, a pickup rolled by. Clay wondered if anyone else had driven by while he was kissing her. If they had, Clay never would have known it. He'd been oblivious to everything but the taste and feel of her.

Andie had her arms folded protectively over her breasts again. Her lips were red and full from the kiss. Her face was flushed.

"Why did you do that?" Her voice was tight.

He felt irritated at her suddenly, for pulling back, for trying to avoid what was going to happen eventually anyway.

"I told you." His voice was harder, perhaps, than it should have been. "Because I want you."

Her mouth had no trace of softness about it now. "Just like that." She flicked a hand in the air. "Out of nowhere. Because you want me."

He looked down at his shoes and then back up at her. "You want me, too."

"Don't change the subject."

"This *is* the subject. I want you. You want me. It's simple, if you'll only—"

"It is not." She tossed an indignant glance heavenward and then glared at him once more. "It's impossible."

"No."

"Good Lord, Clay. We have to *work* together."

"I am very well aware of that."

"You could have fooled me. What's gotten into you?"

You! he wanted to shout at her. *You and your black hair and your wide brown eyes and your scent like flowers and ripe summer fruit.*

But he didn't say that. He said, "I want us to be married."

She stared. "Excuse me?"

"I said, I want to marry you. Right away."

She took another step back from him. "Clay, this is ridiculous. It would never work."

"Oh, yes it will. It will work out just fine."

"Clay." She pitched her voice low, but its intensity made it sound like a shout. "I'm *pregnant,* Clay. And it's not your baby."

"I know. That's one of the reasons, probably the most important reason. For the sake of the baby."

Andie shook her head.

Clay nodded.

She backed away, up the street. "I . . . this is impossible. I can't talk about this now."

"When, then?"

"Don't do this."

"When?"

She glared at him. "I just...right this minute, I *hate* you, Clay Barrett." She sounded very much as she had when they were kids.

Clay was firm, he did not revert to childish taunts. "But you want me. And you'll marry me."

"Not now. I can't think about this now."

"Fine. Tonight, then. We'll talk about it more tonight."

"Oh, God. Tonight."

"Eight o'clock."

"Where?"

"I'll come to your place." No way he was going to tell her to come to his. In the state she was in, she might not show up.

"I can't..."

"Say you'll be there, Andie. Just say that."

"All right." She gave a little frustrated moan. "Oh, how can you do this to me? Everything was worked out. It was all going just fine."

"Say it."

"Damn you."

"Say it."

"I'll be there." And then she turned and ran up the street, all the way to her mother's house.

Andie moved through the rest of her birthday party in a daze, trying to smile and be gracious as the guest of honor, when all she wanted to do was go home.

Go home to her apartment and close all the blinds and sit on her bed and hug her tattered old teddy bear that she'd had since she was a baby.

Clay had *kissed* her.

A real kiss. A man-and-woman kiss.

It wasn't possible.

But it was true.

And, Lord forgive her, she had *liked* it. Liked it more than any kiss she'd ever had in her life.

And then, after that incredible, unforgivable kiss, he'd told her he wanted to marry her.

Marry her.

All her life she'd thought that her watchful, cautious cousin was like a sleeping volcano. Now and then she'd wondered what it would be like if he woke up some day and started spewing fire.

Well, now she knew.

She'd been licked by the flames, swallowed by the heat. It couldn't be true. But it was. Just as Clay had said. She *wanted* him.

It was just a little eerie, actually. Because when she'd blown out the candles on her cake, she'd wished for a good man to stand beside her.

And then, not half an hour later, Clay had asked her to marry him.

Weird. Very weird.

And impossible. Even if Clay *was* a good man. Even if, as he'd so blankly pointed out, she desired him, nothing could come of it. Nothing but trouble.

There was her job to consider, a job she needed and loved. For a woman to desire her boss rarely led to anything but heartache and the unemployment line. And worse than the way her job was suddenly in jeopardy, there was the truth about the baby's father. She could never tell Clay the truth about Jeff. It would kill Clay to know that his best friend was the one.

And Andie knew very well that the family was involved in this. She could read them all like the open books they were. Andie was pregnant and Clay was single and reliable and only related to Andie by adoption.

How perfect, they were all thinking, *Clay and Andie can get married and everything will be fine.* Andie was also reasonably certain, judging by a few oblique remarks her mother had made, that they'd even tried to convince themselves that Clay was the baby's father.

Which was ridiculous, if they'd only open their eyes. If Clay had been the baby's father, he would have married her in a minute. If she'd refused him, he would have bullied and prodded, reasoned and pleaded. He would have kept after her relentlessly until she gave in. Clay was like that. He always faced his duty and did the right thing.

And now, with a little subtle goading from the family, Clay had decided that the right thing would be for him to marry her anyway—even though the baby *wasn't* his.

Oh, she could gladly strangle each and every one of her loving relatives.

Oh, go on with him, honey, her mother had said when Clay had made that strange request that she walk him to his car. As if Andie hadn't seen the gleam in her mother's eyes.

It was too crazy. And impossible, just as she'd tried to tell Clay.

But Clay wouldn't listen to her.

That was always the problem. Clay had never listened to her. Once he decided what he thought was right, he acted on it. And everyone else just had to go along.

Well, Andie had never gone along. And she was not going to go along now.

Tonight, when he came to see her, she would be better prepared. They would have a real discussion of this, like the two adults they were now. Somehow, without revealing the awful truth about Jeff, she would make her pigheaded cousin see reason.

And then, please God, they would go back to the way things had been before.

Chapter Six

When Andie opened her door to Clay that night, her eyes were deep and serious. She wore neither lipstick nor a smile.

She stepped back to let him in. When he moved past her, he didn't miss the care she took not to allow her body to touch his.

"You can hang your coat there." She indicated a row of pegs by the door.

Clay hung his coat and followed her into her small living room.

"Can I get you something?"

"No, thanks."

"Sit down." She gestured at the couch.

He sat where she'd pointed. Andie perched on a chair several feet away.

Clay had his arguments all lined up in his head. But he could see she wanted to speak first. He allowed that.

"Clay, I . . . I'm sorry about the, um, harsh things I said this afternoon. I didn't mean them. Not all of them, anyway. I *don't* hate you. Not really."

"I know that."

She forced a weak smile. "It was just that you shocked me. That kiss. And then saying you wanted to marry me, out of nowhere like that."

"I understand."

One of her slim hands had found a loose thread on the chair arm. Clay watched as she tugged at it, then realized what she was doing and let the thread go.

She spoke again. "I've thought about what you said this afternoon. I really have."

"And?" His stupid heart was in his throat. He swallowed it down.

"And, well, I really don't see how it could work."

Clay gave himself a moment to let her careful refusal sink in. He didn't like it, didn't like the way it made his chest feel tight and his stomach knot up. But it didn't matter. She would marry him in the end. It was what he wanted and it was the right thing. Whatever it took, he would make it happen.

"Why not?" He was proud of how unconcerned he sounded.

She drew in a long breath. "Oh, Clay. Come on. It has to be obvious."

"Fine. Then state the obvious. Please."

"Well." She gave a little nervous cough. "Okay. If you insist."

"I do."

"First, and most important, we aren't in love."

He looked at her for a long time. "Love."

"Yes. Love."

He considered for a moment, framing his argument. Then he spoke. "Of course there's love between us, Andie. We're family, you and me. We work together and we do it damn well. We can build a good life, help each other, *be* there for each other. And we can give your baby two parents to see it all the way to adulthood. That's all the love there needs to be."

Andie wasn't convinced. "No, Clay. That's not enough."

"What else is there?"

She looked away, then back. "You know."

"Tell me."

"Fine. I will." She pulled herself straighter in her chair. "There's a special kind of love that should be there, between a man and a woman when they decide to marry. It's not there with us. You say you love me. But you're not *in* love with me. Are you?"

He tried to contain his impatience, but it was there in his voice when he spoke. "This is a word game, Andie. Nothing more."

"It's not. I want to be in love with the man I marry."

"You'll have love. The only kind that matters."

"It's not enough."

There was a silence, a heated one. She watched him with grim hostility. And her breathing was agitated. Clay thought that he could make this a hell of a lot easier on both of them if he just got up and went over to her and pulled her into his arms. If he did it slowly, she might accept him.

Or he could give in and tell her in so many words that he was in love with her.

Why not, he thought? Why not just say the words she wanted to hear? He cared for her and was willing to do just about anything to see that she was safe and well provided for.

But somehow, those words just wouldn't come. Because in the sense that she meant *in love,* he would be telling a bald-faced lie. There was simply no such thing as the love she thought she wanted. Love like that was just a pretty word for a natural biological urge.

"Clay, please understand." Her soft voice tried to soothe him.

He only bristled more. "Understand what?"

"Don't be angry."

"I'm not."

"Oh, Clay. If I could only make you see. I've made a lot of mistakes. I know I have. But I've also learned a lot. And I really believe that a very special kind of love is important, between a man and a woman, when they begin a life together."

He decided to leave the issue of love alone for right then, since it seemed to be getting them nowhere. "Okay. And what else?"

"What do you mean?"

"What other issues and questions? What else is bothering you?"

"Well, I...I believe there should be honesty, Clay. That honesty between a man and a wife is second only to love."

He regarded her coolly. "Honesty."

"Clay, don't—"

"You're saying you don't think we're being honest with each other. Am I right?"

"Well, I..."

"Say what you mean to say, Andie. Who's lying and what about?"

"It's not a lie. Not really. It's just...about the baby's father." She looked down at her lap and her misery was painful to see.

Clay felt a twinge of guilt again, as he did every time this subject came up around her. He knew the truth, after all. Her closely guarded secret, to him, was no secret at all. He reminded her, "The man is out of your life, isn't he?"

"Yes."

"And out of the baby's life, too?"

"Yes."

"How big is the chance that later, sometime in the future, he'll change his mind?"

She gave him the answer he knew she would give. "Not big. Very small, actually."

"Then why borrow trouble? I'm willing to accept your word about this. The baby will be *our* baby."

Andie stared up at him, a strange expression on her face, hopeful and disbelieving at once. "You would do that? Claim the baby as yours?"

"Yes."

She looked as though she might cry. "Oh, Clay."

"So marry me."

He waited, his heart in his throat. For a moment he actually thought he had convinced her.

But then she sighed and looked at her lap again. "No. I just can't. I know you can't understand that. But it's the way it is. I can't tell you about the baby's father. And I could never marry a man who didn't know the truth. To start out with something like that between us would doom it all right from the first."

Clay studied her bent head. He thought of Jeff, who was dead to him now. And he thought of how he'd sworn to himself that Andie would never have to learn that he knew about Jeff.

He still saw no real reason to tell her the truth. Jeff was the past. And the past would fade to nothing in time. There was no point at all in dwelling on it, in bringing up all the pain and digging around in it for the sake of some noble concept like *honesty*.

What they needed to do was let it go. He saw that clearly. And she would see it soon enough, he was certain.

He stood. "Look. Andie."

Her head shot up. She stared at him, her eyes wide and wary.

He took a step toward her.

She leaned back in her seat. "I don't think you should..."

"What?"

"I, um..."

He stood over her. "Andie." He reached down and took her hand. She let him do that, though her apprehension was plain in every line of her slender body.

He gave a tug. She slowly stood. He backed away a little, in order to give her just enough space that she wouldn't feel she had to cut and run.

She swallowed. "What?"

He felt tenderly toward her suddenly. He knew what she was experiencing. Consciousness of him as a man.

It was a strange, disorienting feeling, he knew. They'd been certain things to each other for almost twenty years. But now they were finding that what they shared was like one of those drawings with an invisible figure hidden within it. You could look for years and never see the hidden figure, but once you saw it, you couldn't *unsee* it. From that moment on, it would always be there.

Gently he whispered, "I won't accept a no."

Her expression became earnest. "You'll have to. It's the only answer, Clay. I'm sorry. Please understand. We have to go back to the way things were."

He shook his head. "We can't do that."

"But we have to."

"We can't."

"Why not?"

"If you insist on saying no, you'll see why not."

"I think we can."

Because he couldn't stop himself, he touched the side of her face with his hand. Her skin was like the petal of a rose. He wanted her mouth again, to taste her mouth.

"Please don't, Clay."

He dropped his hand. Then he turned away. He took the few steps to the sliding glass door that opened onto her minuscule patio. In the window glass, he saw his own shadowed reflection and that of the room behind him.

He was pushing too fast, he knew. He wanted things settled. And he wanted her. Soon.

She was over two months along. And he was greedy for her.

He knew it was crude and thoughtless of him to feel that way, and he certainly would never tell her that. But it was an imperative for him. He wanted to lay a real claim to her, and if they waited too long, the pregnancy could interfere. The thought of having to wait until after the baby came to make love to her set his nerves on edge.

Still, she was not going to tell him yes tonight—that much was painfully clear. He would do them both a service to back off for a while.

She needed to learn firsthand, from day-to-day experience, just what he meant when he said they couldn't go back. Let them work side by side in the office for a few days with this new awareness between them. She'd see soon enough that unsatisfied desire could scrape her nerves raw.

He turned to face her. "Look. I guess there isn't much more to say at this point. Let's leave it for now. You know where I stand on this. I want to marry you. I think we'll be good together as husband and wife. So you think about my offer."

"Clay." She made a small, frustrated sound. "I said no. I meant it. I'm not going to marry you."

"Fine. But there's no law that says you can't change your mind."

"I *won't* change my mind."

"We're talking in circles here."

"Because you won't face the truth." She was glaring at him now, her fists clenched in impotent anger at her sides.

He had the most ridiculous flash of memory at that moment. He saw her at twelve or thirteen, outraged at some imagined injustice he'd done her, her fists clenched at her sides and her face scrunched up in a glare, looking almost exactly as she did right now. Whatever they'd been fighting over, he remembered she'd ended up shouting at him. And he'd shouted right back.

It occurred to him right then that if he didn't get out of there, they would end up yelling at each other like a couple of kids. Either that or he would drag her into his arms and shut her up by covering her mouth with his own. Neither option would be likely to further his case in the long run. He'd better get out of there.

He marched toward her. She cringed back, probably afraid he was going to grab her and do something unforgivable—like kiss her. He couldn't resist tossing her a superior smirk as he strode right by her and out to the little cubicle where his coat was hanging. He grabbed the coat off the hook.

"Good night," he called, triumphantly aloof as he went out the door.

Monday morning at the office, Clay was careful to be strictly professional. He was going to have to wait Andie out. And he was ready for that. They would go on as before, until she realized he was right: they *couldn't* go on as before.

Andie saw his point right away.

But there was no way she was going to admit it to Clay.

And besides, it seemed that they *should* have been able to go on as before. Nothing, really, was any different than it had ever been.

And yet everything had changed in a thousand tiny, irrevocable ways.

Andie was so terribly *aware* of Clay now. And that new awareness affected everything. Clay's mere presence in her place of business messed up her concentration. Even when he was down the hall with his door closed, her silly mind would wander to thoughts of him. All the time now, she'd find herself staring into space with a half-finished letter on the computer screen in front of her, listening with every fiber of her being for the sound of Clay's door being pulled back, for the soft thud of his footfalls as he came out into the hall.

His voice set off alarms inside her. And the sight of him could make her weak.

Clay was a handsome man. She'd always known that. But to Andie, Clay's good looks had been nothing but a fact, like his brown hair and green eyes, his high forehead and his straight nose. She'd never thought twice about them. Not even back in high school, when her girlfriends were always swooning over him.

"Sweet Mother Mary, Clay Barrett's got everything," her best friend Ruth Ann used to sigh. "He's smart, he plays sports, and he's got that dangerous look in his eye." Ruth Ann would give a little shiver. "All that control. That's the thing about Clay Barrett. Just the idea of breaking through all that control."

Andie would groan. "Oh, please . . ."

"Plus he has A-1 fantabulous buns."

"Pass the onion dip, will you?"

"How can you do that? Ask for the onion dip when we're discussing Clay Barrett's buns?"

"It's easy. Pass the onion dip."

"I don't think you're normal, Andrea McCreary."

"I'm normal." Andie had reached across her friend and scooped up the container of dip. "If you knew Clay like I know Clay, you wouldn't give two bits for his buns."

"Try me. I'd *love* to know him like you know him. And you're not even *really* related to him, even though your mother and his mother are sisters. Mother Mary and Joseph, it's the perfect setup. You go to his house for dinner practically every Sunday."

Andie chose a big chip and plowed it through the gooey dip. "Every other Sunday." She stuck the chip in her mouth.

"Oh. Right. And the rest of the Sundays, *he* goes to *your* house. How can you pass up a chance like that? You could be working your wiles on him."

"My *wiles?*" Andie sneered, then chose another chip, shoveled on the dip and popped the delicious morsel into her mouth. "Um. Heaven."

"Like I said, you're not normal. You eat anything you want and stay disgustingly thin. And you don't have a crush on your gorgeous cousin."

"Look," Andie had said around another mouthful of onion dip, "I don't eat anything I want, believe me. I eat too much junk food and then I starve myself when dinner comes around and someday, when I get old, I'll have to take better care of myself. And as far as Clay Barrett goes, it's bad enough I had to grow up with him. God would not be that cruel to make me have a crush on him, too."

Andie groaned when she thought of that long-ago conversation and all the others like it that she and Ruth Ann had shared.

Because all of a sudden, God *was* being that cruel.

And it got in the way of her performance at work, this unforeseen, impossible *crush* she was suffering from. She misplaced folders. She saved letters in the wrong files. She sometimes didn't even hear the little buzzer over the door until the client was standing at the reception counter, clearing his or her throat and waiting for Andie to look up from her computer and notice that someone was there.

And Clay was distant. Distant and irritable. He acted like an adult version of the judgmental tyrant he used to be when they were kids. He watched her. He seemed to be thinking mean things about her. And he rarely cracked a smile.

By the time Andie finally escaped the office at the end of the day and went home, she was a wreck. It was as bad as it had been in January, when she'd realized she was pregnant and didn't have the faintest idea what she was going to do about it. Every day was hell. But at least in January, Clay had been pleasant and reasonably kind while he watched her all the time.

Now, he remained completely detached. He wanted the work done and he wanted it done now and he had no time for a gentle word or a teasing compliment.

Andie remembered very well now why she'd detested him for all those years. He was absolutely heartless when thwarted. Sometimes, when he barked at her for misplacing a file or not getting a letter or a bill out on time, she wanted to just stand up from her computer and yell at him that he was the meanest man she'd ever met, that she hated him and she quit.

But she controlled herself. She remembered the baby. She remembered that there was someone else to think of now, not just herself. She could ride this out. She knew she could.

However, by Thursday night, just five nights after Clay had insisted she marry him, Andie was so depressed that she wondered how she was going to go on. Ruth Ann called to see how she was doing at a little after eight.

"What is the *matter?*" Ruth Ann demanded immediately.

"Nothing."

"Right. I'll be right over."

"Ruth Ann, really, it's not—" But the dial tone was already buzzing in her ear. Ruth Ann had hung up.

The doorbell rang ten minutes later. When Andie opened it, her friend was grinning on the other side.

But then Ruth Ann frowned. "Saint Teresa, what happened? You looked great, and now you look like somebody killed your cat again."

"Thanks."

Ruth Ann stepped inside the door, kicked it closed with her foot and leaned back against it. "Johnny's watching the kids."

"That was nice of him."

"He said to take as long as I wanted. Who woulda thought it, huh? Meadow Valley High's most incorrigible bad actor now deserves a medal as a husband and a daddy." She held up a brown bag. "I come bearing ice cream. Peanut butter caramel mocha fudge. It *has* to be a sin, right?"

"I'm just not hungry."

"Something is definitely wrong." Ruth Ann grabbed Andie's arm, pulled her into the kitchen and dished out the ice cream into bowls. Then she sat opposite Andie and commanded, "There. Eat. And tell Ruth Ann all about it."

And Andie did. Ruth Ann listened the way Ruth Ann always listened, with absolute attention, her pointed chin thrust forward, her eyes bright and alert. When Andie was done, Ruth Ann relaxed a little. She took a big bite of ice cream.

"Well?" Andie asked, when Ruth Ann had swallowed and started to take another bite without saying anything.

"Well, what?" Ruth Ann savored that other bite.

"Well, now that you've heard it, what do you think?"

Ruth Ann clinked her spoon on the edge of her bowl. "You don't want to hear what I think."

"Yes, I do. Tell me."

Ruth Ann set down her spoon. "Do what he wants. Marry him."

"What?"

"You heard me. He won't give up. You know how he is. And you've admitted you've finally seen the light about him."

"What light?"

"That he's *sexy,* you idiot. That he turns you on. I always told you—"

"Spare me. Please."

"You want him. Admit it."

"You're beginning to sound a lot like him, Ruth Ann."

"Sometimes the truth is painful to deal with, from any source."

"Ruth Ann. His best friend was the father of my baby. He doesn't know that. I want a real marriage, if I ever have one. A marriage like you've got. Based on love and trust. I can't marry a man who doesn't already know and accept the truth about my baby."

"Fine. So tell him the truth."

"You *are* kidding."

"No. The way it looks from my chair, you don't have a lot of options. How long do you think you're gonna last, working for him every day and having this unsettled *thing* between you? It's only been, what? Four days, and you look almost as bad as you did before you told him you were pregnant and got that out of the way. You should either quit your job—not a terrific choice, I gotta admit, at this point in your life—or tell him what you're afraid to tell him and then wing it from there. You're in deadlock right now, kiddo. It's an ugly place to be."

"But it will *hurt* him, if I tell him. It will hurt him so badly."

"For a woman who can't stand that man, you sure are worried about how bad you're gonna hurt him."

"I never said I couldn't stand him."

"For all the years while we were growing up, that's *all* you said."

"That was then. Things change."

"Oh, really? And anyway, you should have thought of all this before you spent the night with that Jeff character."

Andie looked down at her bowl of melting ice cream. There was nothing to say to that. Ruth Ann was right.

"Didn't I warn you that you'd end up in trouble with some smooth-talkin' out-of-town guy? You were always too picky, you didn't get yourself any experience and then—"

Andie's head shot up. "Look who's talking. You were a virgin on your wedding night—we both know it."

"I was eighteen on my wedding night and a good Catholic girl. I had a right to be a virgin."

Andie looked down at the table again. "This is a stupid argument. I did what I did. And now I have to deal with the consequences."

Ruth Ann was quiet, then she made a soothing sound. "Well, you're right. You're doing the best you can. I'm sorry if I'm too rough on you."

Andie sighed. "I just don't know what to do. If Clay finds out, he'll kill Jeff."

"It's a thought. I could kill him myself, actually."

"Oh, stop it. I was as much at fault for what happened as Jeff was."

"Fine. I still hate the jerk's guts. Want more ice cream?"

"No, thanks."

"I believe I will have just one more little scoop." Ruth Ann went to the refrigerator and dished herself out another bowlful. "Well, like I said, your options are limited. And you can't control what Clay will do." Ruth Ann closed the carton and put it away. "You sure you can't live with just marrying him and *not* telling him?" She licked the serving spoon, considering. "I mean, after all, things really are *finito* between you and the best friend. It's not like you're pining away for him or anything."

Andie looked at her friend in blank disbelief. "Oh, that's a great idea. And then what will I do when Clay and I are married and the baby's been born and Clay wants us to fly down to Los Angeles and visit his best pal, Jeff?"

"Yuck." Ruth Ann set the serving spoon in the sink and began eating from her bowl. "You're right. Not good. Maybe looking for another job *is* the only real choice, after all."

Andie leaned her chin on her hand. She felt so tired. The last thing she wanted to do was go looking for another place to work. But if she was going to have to do it, she should do it right away. She wasn't showing yet, but she would be soon enough. Who would hire a woman who'd be needing maternity leave right away? She'd probably end up working a series of temp jobs for less pay and no benefits, at least until she'd had the baby and was back on her feet again.

And speaking of benefits, what about her insurance? Could she keep it if she left Barrett & Co.? And if she did, how much would it end up costing her a month? She should look into that. Given that she managed to find another job, any insurance she got from it wouldn't go into effect for a while. And then it probably wouldn't cover her having the baby.

Which would mean the family would end up stepping in to take up the slack. She didn't want them to do that. She didn't want them to end up picking up the tab for a choice that was all her own. She didn't want to burden them, and she didn't want to watch them all shake their heads knowingly and whisper that they'd seen this coming all along.

She wanted them to *admire* her the way they admired Clay. So that her child could be proud of her. So that her child could look at her with confidence and feel safe and protected, the way Andie had been safe and protected while she was growing up.

Oh, it was all just a nightmare. A nightmare, any way she turned.

Everything had been all worked out. Things were going just great.

And then Clay had to go and decide to marry her. And her whole fragile little life was turned upside down all over again.

Andie thought of her savings account, which had been growing steadily the past couple of years. With the money Jeff had sent and the bonus from Clay, she now had very close to twelve thousand dollars. She'd been saving for a house of her own, but of course now that would have to be put off.

Oh, she had been such a foolish dreamer of a girl. She'd wasted too many years, drifting, not applying herself. Having fun.

She hadn't earned the grades in high school to get into a really good college. Yet she hadn't minded, really. Life was easy and every day held something to delight her. In summer, there were trips to the river with her friends and waterskiing at the local reservoir. And in winter, there was snowmobiling and cross-country skiing and warm fires waiting when she came in from the snow. She'd found a job as a waitress that paid well enough. And she'd enjoyed herself thoroughly.

By the time she began to think she should do something with her life, she was in her twenties. She'd buckled down then, going to junior college and then to a business school.

Then Uncle Don's longtime office manager had decided to retire. Uncle Don had offered Andie the job. Andie had hesitated at first. She knew that someday Clay would return and the old animosity between them might ruin things. But Uncle Don had offered to pay her very well. The benefits were great, too. And Clay wasn't going to come home for years, anyway. So Andie had stepped in, surprising everyone with her efficiency and her willingness to work. She'd loved the job, especially after the old office manager left and she could run things all on her own.

Then Uncle Don had suffered his heart attack. Clay had come back ahead of schedule.

Those first months with Clay as her boss had been a rough time for Andie. She'd known she would have to prove herself all over again to him. And she'd done it. Clay had discovered how good she was, in spite of his prejudices against her.

But deep down, she'd resented having to prove her competence to the rival of her teenage years. And maybe what had happened on New Year's Eve was partly because of that. Because her feelings had grown so tangled since Clay had come home. Because all of her accomplishments the past few years were minor compared to his. Because every time she looked at him, she felt edgy and unhappy and unsatisfied with herself. And yet she hadn't been able to let her feelings out. To do that might have cost her her job.

"Come on," Ruth Ann suggested, cutting through Andie's unhappy thoughts, "let's see if there's a decent tearjerker on cable."

"Oh, Ruthie. Watching a movie is not going to solve my problem."

"No, but your problem is not going to be solved tonight, anyway. So you might as well try to forget it for an hour or two. Come on. A little oblivion is good for a person."

"Oh, Ruthie . . ."

"Come on." Ruth Ann grabbed Andie's hand and pulled her to her feet. "Get in there and find the viewer's guide. I'll make the popcorn."

Since tearjerkers turned out to be in short supply, they watched *The Terminator*. Ruth Ann sat on one end of the couch, squealing between handfuls of popcorn, as Arnold Schwarzenegger cut a swathe through Los Angeles.

Andie sat quietly, hardly aware of what she was watching. By the time the terminator entered the police station and announced, "I'll be back," Andie had made a decision.

She would talk to Clay tomorrow and tell him she was going to be leaving her job.

Chapter Seven

"Close the door." Clay's voice was deadly calm.

Andie shut the door to Clay's office, though there was really no need. It was six-thirty at night and they were alone in the building.

"Now say that one more time, please." He was sitting at the big mahogany desk that had been his father's.

She dragged in a deep breath. "I said, this is not working out for me. I'm giving notice. I'll stay two weeks to help you find someone else and then—"

He stood. "It's the middle of March."

"I know that."

"This is an accounting firm. You'll be leaving at precisely the busiest two weeks of the year."

"It can't be helped."

Clay swore crudely and succinctly. "Oh, yes it can."

"Time is running out for me, Clay. If I want to find another position before the baby's born, I have to start looking right away."

"You're not quitting. You're going nowhere."

Andie gaped at him. "Pardon me? I don't believe that you said that."

"Believe it. It's true. You're not quitting."

"I am."

"You're not."

"This is ridiculous."

"You're damned right it is. What the hell goes through that mind of yours? You *need* this job—and this company needs you."

"Well, thank you for admitting that I'm needed around here. You could have fooled me the past few days."

"The past few days have been difficult. For both of us. I warned you that they would be." Clay spoke very slowly, like someone trying to reason with an insane person.

Andie leaned back against the door she'd just shut, feeling the tiredness in every inch of her body. "I can't do this. I can't *stand* this. It isn't good for me. And it can't be good for my baby."

"Then marry me."

Tears filled Andie's eyes. She willed them back. She was not going to be some silly, weepy female over this. She'd made the best choice of a bad lot. And he would not dissuade her from what had to be done.

She straightened, pulling her shoulders up. "No, Clay. It won't work."

"It will." Slowly, he came around the desk toward her.

"Clay, don't . . ."

"Don't what?"

"You know what."

"No. Tell me."

She watched him approaching. Her body, so totally exhausted just a moment ago, was suddenly humming, pulsing with a restless, hot kind of energy.

"Tell me." Clay's eyes were green fire. She couldn't stop looking into them.

Andie swallowed. "I . . ."

And then he was right there. So close that she could feel his body heat.

"This isn't fair." Her voice held no conviction at all.

"I know." Clay's tone was gentle now. He cupped her chin in his hand. His skin burned her. All her senses centered down to the touch of his flesh against hers. "It's just the way it is. Maybe the way it's always been. Did you ever think about that?"

Andie's mind had slowed; she couldn't think. "About what?"

Clay lowered his head just enough to brush his lips across hers. Down below, she went liquid. It was crazy. She softly moaned.

"About you and me," Clay whispered against her mouth. "Fighting. Enemies for all those years. Your dad said something. Love and hate are very close. . . ."

"You don't believe in love."

"That's right. I don't. I want to kiss you. I want to be inside you."

Andie gasped, both aroused and shocked at the bluntness of his words. "I don't . . ."

"Yes, you do. You want it. With me. Just like I want it with you. There's no point in your quitting. This will not go away."

"It might."

"It won't. It took too long. Years and years building up. And now it's not something we can get over in a day, or a week, a few months."

"How do you know this?"

"I just do. It will take a very long time, I think."

"It will?"

Clay nodded. And then he wrapped his fingers lightly around her neck. "Your skin is so soft. The other night, I remember thinking it was like rose petals."

"Oh, Clay. This is not how I—"

"Shh. I know. I wasn't going to do this, either. Until I had your agreement to marry me. But here I am. Breaking my promise to myself. I should be ashamed. But I'm not."

He looked so very vulnerable then that she smiled before she could stop herself.

"Ah," he sighed. "A smile. I saw that. I've missed your smiles."

"You have?"

"Absolutely. It's been so grim around here without them."

"But it's because of you that I've been—"

"Shh, don't argue. Don't talk at all."

"But I—"

He didn't let her finish. His mouth closed over hers, taking her denials into himself.

Andie sighed, already open for him. She felt his tongue breach the soft barrier of her lips and she didn't even pretend to evade it. She welcomed it, allowing him to explore her in this intimate way, even daring to meet his tongue with a few shy thrusts of her own.

Clay lifted his mouth enough to whisper, "Yes," and then he slanted his lips the other way and kissed her some more.

His hand strayed downward, to the bow at the collar of her silk blouse. He pulled the ends of the bow and she heard a soft whisking sound as it slithered loose. Then he smoothed the tails open and slipped the collar button from its hole.

Andie's nipples ached, pebbling to attention as he lightly brushed them through her clothing. Her knees could hardly hold her up. She was grateful for the nice solid door to lean against.

Clay slipped the next button free and then the next, his mouth playing over hers all the while. And then he was pulling the blouse free of her skirt, pushing it gently off her shoulders.

The blouse floated to the floor. He eased down the straps of her slip and then did the same with her bra straps, guiding them off her shoulders. Her bra fell away.

It came to her, distantly, that she was standing in Clay's office naked to the waist. He pulled her close and the tender skin of her breasts was pressed against the wool jacket of his suit. Her nipples, already aching, hardened even more. He rubbed himself against her, imprinting his body onto hers. She felt his desire through all the layers of their clothing.

"Oh, Clay..."

Andie nuzzled her head against the crook of his shoulder, aware of his scent. She put her lips to his strong neck, and parted them just enough that she tasted his skin.

Clay brought his hands between them, feeling for her breasts. He cupped them and rubbed the nipples between his fingers. She let her head fall back as she moaned.

But then, for no reason she could comprehend, he was gripping her shoulders, pushing her away, holding her at arm's length.

"What?" Andie murmured, confused, forcing herself to open her eyes and see what he wanted.

Clay's expression was unreadable. He looked at her face, her neck, her shoulders, her breasts. And then he muttered something so low that she couldn't make out the words.

Andie was dazed, yearning. She reached for him, wondering vaguely what was happening, wanting him close again, wanting his wonderful caresses never to stop.

Clay gripped her shoulders harder, holding her even farther away from him. "Andie."

She blinked. "What?"

"Come home with me tonight."

She blinked again. It was all too fast for her. She had to get away from him, get a moment to collect herself. But there was nowhere to go, so she pressed her body harder against the door. And then she slowly bent to retrieve her blouse and bra.

Clay took a step back, picking up her signal for space and acquiescing to it. He waited while she straightened her clothing and buttoned her blouse.

When she was covered, she met his eyes. "I came in here to tell you I quit. And then, all of a sudden, you were kissing me." Chagrin washed over her. "I let you kiss me."

"You did more than that. You kissed me back. Come home with me."

She looked at him, wanting him. Knowing that what he had said earlier was right. There was a very good chance she would *always* want him. From now on.

What was between them was so powerful. It seemed, in this moment of piercing desire, to have always been. Her battles with Clay were so much a part of who she was that she would not be herself had she not known him, fought him, envied him, raged at him.

"Come home with me. We'll make love. It will diffuse some of the tension, at the very least. And afterward, we'll talk."

"There's nothing to talk about."

"We'll see. But in any case, we'll have tonight."

"I don't see how going home with you could make things anything but worse."

"Who's the cautious one now?" He closed the distance between them again. He put his hands on her shoulders once more and gently rubbed through the silk of her blouse. "It would have happened right here. On the rug. Or against the door. I stopped it. You know I did. Show me the guts I know you have. Make it a conscious choice to come with me now. Otherwise, next time I won't stop it. I'll let it happen all the way, wherever we are."

Andie started to say, I won't let it happen again. But that would have been such a blatant lie, she couldn't quite get it out of her mouth.

He was right. It *would* happen again. She was absolutely starved for him. All he'd have to do was what he'd done tonight. Get her alone. Approach her slowly and deliberately. She would beg him to kiss her, to touch her, to take her yearning full circle to total fulfillment.

Oh, sweet Lord, it was so strange. So bewildering. Andie had waited all of her life, turned away every man but Jeff Kirkland. She'd *known* that just what was happening now would happen someday, that there would be a man who could set her on fire with just a touch. It was one of the most basic of her girlhood dreams.

She'd never given up that dream. Not until a few months ago, when it had begun to seem somehow childish and unreal. A romantic fantasy that was never going to come true.

It had made her sad, the death of that dream. She had mourned it. She'd even told Jeff Kirkland about it, on New Year's Eve.

Clay demanded, "What are you thinking about?"

Andie sighed. "This is impossible. All of it."

"So forget it. Forget thinking. For now. Come home with me."

Andie searched his green eyes. "Oh, Clay. Please tell me this is not another stupid move I'm making, another one of my crazy mistakes."

"That's easy." His voice was firm. "This is not a stupid move. This is what we both want and what will happen eventually, anyway. Come home with me."

Andie thought about her dream again. That at last, the man in her dream had a face: Clay's face. But in her dream, the man said he loved her. Clay didn't love her, not in the way that she longed to be loved. Clay wanted her and would marry her and would take her baby as his own.

And really, shouldn't that be enough?

Maybe he was right. Maybe it was enough. But why did it feel as if there was some great big hole in the center of all of it, then?

And what about her own heart? Was she in love with Clay?

Oh, sweet heaven, she feared that perhaps she was. Yet something inside her held back from that—from admitting to a woman's love for him.

In her life, he'd always been so powerful. It had seemed to Andie that her cousin always got his way. If she gave him her heart, he'd have everything. She'd be completely at his mercy then, far below him, looking up.

And he was so self-contained. Aunt Della always said that Clay never revealed his heart. Aunt Della thought it was because of the difficulties of his early years, because he'd been hurt and alone and had to turn into himself to survive.

Andie could sympathize with that. But could she live with a man who was like that? How would she ever talk to him about the things that mattered, about the things that hurt?

Like Jeff.

"What are you thinking?"

She veered away from the ugly truth to a more general answer. "A thousand things. You. Me. The family. The family wants us to get together. You know that, don't you?''

He shrugged. "Yes."

"You'd do anything for them, wouldn't you?" She tried not to sound bitter.

Clay was unfazed. "Yes, I would, to a point. But I wouldn't marry a woman I didn't want. Not even for the family's sake."

"For some strange reason, I believe you."

"Because I'm telling the truth. Now, give me your answer. Say you'll come home with me."

"You are relentless."

"No argument. Come home with me."

"Nothing can come of it."

"Think that if you want to. But come home with me."

Andie hovered on the edge of a decision for one more moment, wondering how Clay could be so totally focused, so utterly unswerving in the pursuit of his goal. He simply would not give up.

And she was so tired. She wanted to surrender, to go with him to his house and know what it was at last, to share the greatest intimacy with the man from her dream.

If it all fell apart after tonight—which it was bound to do—at least she would have had that much.

She was slumped rather pitifully against the door. She made herself stand straight.

"Well?"

She gave him what he wanted. "All right, Clay. I'll go home with you."

She watched the heat of triumph flare in his eyes. "Good. Let's get out of here."

Chapter Eight

The room lay in shadow. Andrea stood in the door to the hall and looked toward a glass door that led onto a deck. Beyond the deck was the huge, dark, star-scattered sky and the black shapes of distant hills. A sliver of moon hung just above the hills.

It was a beautiful view, Andrea thought. Lucky Clay, to go to sleep every night in a place such as this.

Clay stood behind her. Light as a breath, his hands rubbed her arms. She felt the touch of his mouth at her nape and shivered as his lips caressed her.

Andrea leaned back a little, her body giving a sensual signal to which Clay's arms instantly responded. He pulled her close so she felt him more fully against her and his hands came around her, seeking and finding her breasts.

Andrea moaned. Clay cupped her breasts, felt for the response of the nipples and then rubbed them, so they hardened more through the fabric of her clothing. And then his hands were on the bow at her neck, pulling it loose, slipping buttons free. The front of her blouse fell open. He took it from behind and peeled it away. As he had in the office, he began sliding down straps, getting her underclothes out of his way.

Slowly and with great care, he undressed her. As he removed her clothes, he pressed his body against her back. He kissed her neck and caressed her in long, gentle strokes, making her burn hotter and then hotter still.

The moment came when she was naked. Her clothes were over there and she was over here. Clay turned her so she faced him and then he guided her backward to the bed. He pushed her down. His eyes were burning her again.

Clay backed away from her to turn on a light, just a little one, in a corner. By its soft glow, she could see him. And he could see her. He still wore all his clothes, except for his jacket, which he had shed with his coat downstairs. He approached the bed once more.

When he stood over her, she reached for the buttons of his shirt. But then he knelt on the bed beside her and put his hand on her, there, in her most secret place.

Andrea gasped, shocked. And then she realized how totally she was aroused. She could feel her own wetness. She was like a river down there.

"Yes," Clay said softly. He began to move his hand.

Andrea cried aloud. Her body responded, found the rhythm he was showing her. Nothing else mattered but the magic of his stroking hand. She closed her eyes, sure she would faint, it was so glorious. And all he did was touch her, in this way that should have embarrassed her, but only made her want to beg for more.

Clay said, "You're ready."

Andrea moaned and lifted her hips again. And then his hand went still. She opened her eyes a little and saw that he was pulling off his tie, unbuttoning his shirt.

She rose up enough to help him, though it meant she lost the fabulous intimate caress of his hand. She didn't care. She knew what he hungered for. And she wanted it, too.

It was crucial, essential. He had to be pressed to her, naked as she was. He had to be inside her. Now.

Sooner than now....

Andrea shoved Clay's shirt off his shoulders, helped him tear it off his arms. Swiftly they pulled at his clothes together, getting rid of them, getting them off and away.

And then he rose over her. Oh, he was so wonderful to see. The powerful, sculpted shoulders, the strong arms, the hard, deep chest. His manhood jutted out from the silky nest of brown hair.

Slowly Clay lowered himself upon her. She felt the satiny length of him going in. And it was everything. It was what she had always dreamed. The man of her impossible girlhood fantasies. Made flesh.

He was all the way in. It was the most marvelous, fulfilling ache Andie had ever known. She tried to move.

But he didn't let her. He levered up on his hands and held her fast with his body.

Andie licked her lips. They were so dry. She would die if he didn't let her move.

Clay looked down at her, pushed against her one sweet, tantalizing thrust. He pulled back. And then he groaned. And his face went softer. He slid deep into her once more. She lifted her hips to better receive him.

And at last, he was moving, pushing in and out in long, delicious strokes.

It was such heaven. Oh, she had always known that it could be like this. Her whole body was shimmering. The fulfillment was building.

Andrea longed for the feel of him along the length of her. She lifted her arms, tried to pull him close.

"No," he said. "I want to watch you. I want to see your face." His hips kept moving, the length of him going in and slowly, so slowly, pulling back out.

She felt frantic, so hungry, so needful. She was reaching, reaching . . .

And he was murmuring things, little hot urgent things. She moved faster. He moved with her, picking up each of her body's signals, before she could send them, it seemed.

She reached for him again. And when he still wouldn't come down to her, she stroked his shoulders and the hot, smooth, powerful flesh of his chest. Her fingers moved over him, swift as the wings of a butterfly, learning every contour, committing him to memory.

She had always known him. She had *never* known him. . . .

And then it happened. A pulsing. An expanding and a rippling outward of sensation. Andrea cried out.

Clay whispered, "Yes."

The pulsing went on, to encompass all that she was, to free her for the briefest eternity from her doubts and her unhappiness and from all that remained unsaid and unde- cided.

Somewhere in the middle of it, Clay was caught up, too. She felt him push strongly into her, a movement of his own need, his own hunger that had claimed him at last.

He groaned, a sound of both pleasure and pain. He thrust once more. They both held absolutely still.

She dared to look at him. He met her eyes. The pulsing went on and on.

They whispered "Yes" in unison.

A moment. Forever. And then a gentle fading. Stark wonder became a kind of glow.

Clay sighed. He lowered himself carefully upon her. She welcomed the warmth and hardness of him against her slowing heart.

Gently he rolled to the side, holding her with him, so that they lay facing each other, still joined, arms and legs entwined. He stroked her damp hair and kissed her moist cheek. Andrea cuddled up closer to him, curling her arms against his chest, wrapping him tighter with her legs.

It came to her that something wonderful had happened; she was completely at peace.

Clay said in a whisper that was tired, yet triumphant, "Now you're *both* mine."

She knew what he meant. Both herself and the baby. And she had no desire to argue with him. Perhaps his claim was true. In any case, she understood right then that what had just happened changed everything.

Clay went on gently stroking her hair. For the first time in days Andrea felt totally relaxed. She felt safe. It was okay to give in to exhaustion. She drifted off to sleep.

When Andrea awoke the room was flooded with daylight. She was warm and cozy under the covers. And she was alone.

She sat up and looked for a clock, finding one on the stand on the opposite side of the bed. It was after ten in the morning. She had slept for more than twelve hours.

She stretched and realized she felt quite rested. Her stomach growled. She was starved. She also had to answer nature's call. Badly.

She smiled as she saw the man's robe Clay had left for her at the foot of the bed. Then she tossed back the covers and jumped from the bed, grabbing up the robe and shoving her arms into it as she ran for the master bath.

After relieving herself, she left the private stall that housed the commode and went back out to the main part of the big bathroom. She washed her hands in the sink and stood before the wall-to-wall mirror to run one of Clay's brushes through the wild tangle of her hair.

Her stomach growled again. She really was starved. But aside from hunger, she felt just fine. No queasiness at all. Her morning sickness, which had never confined itself to the morning at all, had been fading for the past week or two. She wasn't the least bit sad to see it go.

Andie turned sideways in the mirror, looking at her stomach. In a feminine gesture as old as motherhood, she put her hand there. It was still flat, nothing showing at all through the heavy bulk of Clay's robe. There was, however, a slight roundness when she was nude.

Nude. Andie blushed a little, thinking of the night before. Clay had been careful with her, in spite of the intensity of what they'd shared. Careful for the baby's sake.

Andie smiled, a dreamy smile. She probably shouldn't feel so wonderful. The only thing that had happened was good sex.

But then, since she'd never had good sex before, she supposed she had a right to feel a little wonderful about it.

"You're awake."

With a small exclamation of surprise, Andie shifted her glance to see Clay in the mirror. He was leaning in the doorway to the bedroom, wearing jeans and a snug, dark blue T-shirt, watching her.

She set down the brush and turned to him, tightening the sash of the robe. "How long have you been standing there?"

He was grinning. "Long enough."

"It's not nice to spy on people."

"I know." He contrived a remorseful expression, though she knew very well he wasn't the least contrite.

"Then why do you do it?"

His beautiful shoulders lifted in a shrug. "Because I've always done it. At least, where you're concerned."

"That's no reason."

"I know."

She planted her hands on her hips, feeling devilish, feeling really good. "How am I going to start an argument with you if you refuse to be goaded?"

He left the doorway then and came toward her. "I don't know. Maybe we'll just have to forget about arguing for now."

Her body seemed to be humming again, the way it had been last night. "That wouldn't be normal. We *always* argue."

He was less than an arm's distance away. He reached out and took the sash of the robe from her fingers. He gave a tug.

She landed against his chest with a soft little sigh. "Don't we?" she prompted, since he had said nothing.

"Don't we what? I forgot what we were talking about." He lowered his mouth and kissed her, slowly, sweetly and thoroughly. Andie forgot what they'd been talking about, too, as she slid her hands up to link around his neck.

When the kiss ended he continued to hold her close, stroking her hair and her back. "Hungry?" He breathed the word against her temple.

She pulled back, though she stayed in the circle of his arms. "Am I ever. I could eat your tractor. Have you eaten?"

"Hours ago."

"You should have woken me up."

"No, I shouldn't. You needed the sleep. Want breakfast?"

"Yes, and a shower."

"In which order?"

"I don't care."

"Go ahead and shower. I'll cook you some eggs."

"Three. Over easy. And toast. With butter and jam."

* * *

Andrea's eggs were waiting when she came downstairs dressed in her rumpled skirt and blouse from the night before.

Clay cast a glance at her clothes. She read the look. He was wondering if she was planning to leave as soon as she ate. But he didn't ask her about it. And she was glad he didn't. Because she didn't know yet just what she was going to do.

"I heated some water," he said. "For your tea."

It touched her that he had noticed she wasn't drinking coffee anymore. But maybe that was silly, for her to be touched about that. Of course Clay would notice. He noticed *everything*, always had.

"Thank you." Andie sat down and spread her napkin on her lap.

"I only have regular tea, though, not that peppermint kind you drink at work."

"Regular tea is fine." She picked up her fork and started to eat. It was so *good*. She forced herself to eat slowly so she wouldn't end up feeling nauseated, after all.

Clay poured the hot water over a tea bag and placed the cup at her side. Then he poured himself some coffee and sat opposite her chair.

After Andie had finished two of the eggs and half of the toast, the sharp edge of her hunger was blunted. She savored the rest of the meal. At last, she pushed the plate away.

"That was wonderful."

He took a sip from his coffee. His eyes were serious.

She knew what was coming. "Oh, Clay."

"We have to talk about it."

"No. We don't. Not right now."

He shook his head. "Andie, Andie. What is it with you? Never do today what you can put off till tomorrow?"

There was a window beside the breakfast table. Andie looked out over the lower deck, over the hillside that sloped away beneath the house and the gnarled live oaks that clung there.

"Look at me, Andie."

She did as he demanded. And took issue with his analysis of her. "I'm not really like that, not about most things. I'm not a procrastinator anymore. If you're going to judge me, please judge me as I am, not as I used to be."

"Fair enough. But still, about this particular subject you *are* putting me off."

She rubbed her eyes. "Maybe. I don't know. I admit, since last night . . ."

"What?"

"I feel differently."

He leaned on the table. The intensity in him came at her like waves of heat from an oven. She knew the strength of his will and the way he was holding himself in check. "Differently, how?"

"I feel kind of hopeful."

"About you and me?"

"Yes." She found she was blushing. "I, um, never felt anything like that before."

He was puzzled. "You never felt hopeful before?"

"No. I mean I never felt anything like what happened last night."

"Good."

Andie gave a little cough, because her throat felt dry. "It looks like, if nothing else, we could get along in bed."

Clay nodded, waiting. And when she said nothing more, he prompted, "So what are you saying, then?"

Andrea waved a hand. "Oh, Clay. Maybe I don't know what I'm saying." She thought of those three little words, *I love you,* which he'd never said. She decided she could live without them. She felt, since last night, that he was hers in a deep and complete way. That he'd always been hers. As she was his. She was finally woman enough to accept that.

And to accept him.

And besides, eternal optimist that she was, she could still hope that he might change someday. That he'd allow himself to believe in love and to tell her he loved her. And then she might have the nerve to show her deepest heart to him as well.

"Andie." The sound was impatient. "Talk to me."

"I'm trying."

"Try harder."

"Don't push me."

Only one thing held her back. The truth about Jeff Kirkland. She could marry without words of love. But she could not marry Clay unless he knew the truth about Jeff.

It would hurt him to know. And who could tell exactly how he might react? Knowing Clay, she thought he might insist on confronting Jeff. That wouldn't be good.

But it would be worse for Clay *not* to know. Jeff was his friend. The baby could look like Jeff. Or someday, God help them, Jeff might change his mind and want into the life of the child he'd helped create.

"Andie."

"All right, Clay."

"All right, what?"

"All right, I'll marry you."

He stared at her, exultant. And then his eyes narrowed. "But what?"

"You know me so well."

"But what?"

Andrea closed her eyes, drew in a breath and then gazed at Clay squarely once more. "But we have to talk about the baby's father."

"No, we don't."

"We do. Or there won't be any marriage. You can be as persistent as you want. But I won't back down about this. You have to know."

"What?" The word burst out of him. "What do I have to know? You want to tell me you still *love* him? Is that it? You still *love* the bastard who made a baby with you and then just walked away?"

"No, Clay. That's not what I want to tell you at all."

Now he was the one drawing in a deep breath. Andrea watched him calm himself. "Then what?"

"You have to know who the man was, Clay. I won't marry you with this lie between us."

He looked wary. "Now you *want* to tell me who he was?"

"When before I said I *couldn't,* I know. You'll understand. Once you know."

Clay was watching her very closely. He had the strangest expression on his face.

And all of a sudden, *she* understood. She gaped at him and then she murmured, "You already know."

Chapter Nine

"How long?" Andie demanded. "How long have you known?"

"Andie." His voice was coaxing. "Settle down."

She wouldn't be coaxed. "How long?"

"Hell. For a while. A few weeks."

"A few weeks." She repeated his words numbly. Then she shook her head. "All this time. I've been worried, knowing I could never tell you, scared to death you might find out someday. And while I've been stewing, you've known all along."

"Yes."

"That Monday morning three weeks ago, when you came in with your face all battered and tried to tell me you fell off your tractor—"

"I'd been to see Jeff. Yes."

"And he beat you up?"

Clay grunted. "Let's say we beat each other up."

Andie found she couldn't sit still. She stood. "You fought. You had an actual, physical fight."

"Yeah."

"What happened? You tell me. All of it."

Clay shifted in his chair, looking miserable. But he did explain. "Damn it, Andie. I'm not blind. And I can count. As soon as you said the baby was due in September, I started thinking about Jeff. And about New Year's Eve, when we all went to that party at Ruth Ann and Johnny's and you and Jeff left together."

"How did you know I left with Jeff? You and your date were gone long before that."

"Jeff told me. He didn't come back to my place until daybreak. And I asked him where he'd been. He said he took you home."

"And what else?"

"I don't remember exactly. Some story about driving around, thinking. He said he'd made up his mind that he wanted to go back to Madeline, if she'd have him. And he did. He went back to L.A. that day."

Andie still couldn't believe this. "So you suspected it was Jeff from the first?"

"Yeah."

"Why didn't you ask *me?*"

"Come on, Andie. The night you told me you were pregnant, you said you'd never tell me who the father was. I knew I wasn't going to get anything out of you. So I went to Jeff. I flew down there and we drove out to the beach together and I asked him point-blank if the baby was his. He admitted it was true."

"What else?"

"He said you wanted to raise the baby on your own and that that was fine with him. All he really cared about was that Madeline wouldn't have to know."

"And?"

"And so I told him I never wanted to see him again. That he was dead to me. He accepted that. And then he punched me. And we fought."

"*He* punched *you?*"

"It was a favor. Never mind. You'd have to be a man."

"Thank God I'm not. Who else knows?"

He snorted. "Knowing you, probably Ruth Ann."

"Very funny. I mean, who else have *you* told?"

"No one. Come on, Andie. Who would I tell? And why the hell would I *want* to tell anyone?"

Andie was still standing, but she put her hands on the table and leaned toward him. She demanded, "What about the family?"

"The family least of all."

Andie straightened, relieved.

He went on. "I think that the family believes the baby is mine." His eyes made a slow, knowing pass from her face to her belly and back up. "And that's just fine with me. As far as I'm concerned, the baby *is* mine. From last night on."

Andie stared at him. She still hadn't fully absorbed the fact that the secret she'd so carefully kept from him was no secret at all. He'd known all along. He'd already confronted Jeff. The worst had happened and she hadn't even realized it was going on.

Her knees felt funny, as if they might not continue to hold her up. And yet she couldn't stay still. She had to move. Just to give herself something to do, she picked up her dirty plate and flatware and carried it all to the sink.

Hastily, her fingers feeling awkward and thick, she rinsed the plate, the fork and the knife and bent to put them in the dishwasher. When she straightened again, Clay was behind her.

He laid his hands on her shoulders and spoke gently against her ear. "Look. It's out now. There's no more secret, no more lie. Can't we go on from here?"

"Oh, Clay." She turned until she could see his eyes. "I don't know. He's your best friend."

"He *was* my friend. But some things can't be forgiven. He's dead to me now."

Andie shivered. "I don't know how you can do that—just cut him from your life like that."

He made a scoffing sound. "*You've* done it." He looked at her sideways. "Haven't you?"

"Yes."

"Then why shouldn't I?"

She gently put his hands from her shoulders and moved away. "It's different for me."

"No, it's not." He spoke from behind her.

She turned to face him. "It is. I only knew him for a couple of weeks over a holiday. I behaved...foolishly with him. I only feel relief when I think that I'll probably never see him again. He wasn't my friend. I had no history with him."

"What the hell are you getting at?"

"That Jeff Kirkland is a very special person in your life. And he's not in mine."

"That's ridiculous."

"Oh, Clay. Stop it. You actually had *fun* with him. I saw you. I'd never seen you laugh the way you did with him. It...astonished me. I saw you in a whole new light, during those two weeks when Jeff was here."

"So?"

"So it's my fault that your friendship is destroyed."

"It's not your fault."

"At the least, it's half my fault."

"He took advantage of you. He—"

"No. Don't you dare say that. Don't you dare try to make me into Jeff Kirkland's victim. I wasn't. I did what I did of my own free will."

"Fine. And so did he. And what he did, I will never be able to forgive. He created a baby, and then he just walked away. A man like that is no man. Even if you don't marry me, it will make no difference as far as my relationship with Jeff is concerned. I'll never see him again."

Andie shook her head. She felt such sadness. "Oh, Clay. If you can't forgive *him,* how will you ever forgive *me?*"

"What the hell's the matter with you? Do you *want* me to forgive him?"

"I don't know." She backed up against the L of the kitchen counter and leaned there. "I just can't help thinking that if I weren't in the picture, Jeff would still be your friend."

"He had choices, Andie."

"So did I."

Clay moved toward her. "We're not getting anywhere with this. It's over. He's out of our lives. The best thing we can do now is go on. Make a good life together, give the baby the chance he or she deserves."

"I just don't—"

"Look around you." He made a wide gesture with his hand. "This house has four bedrooms and a study. And plenty of room outside for kids to grow in. I made some pretty good money those last couple of years with Stanley, Beeson and Means and I've used it wisely, I promise you. Half of all I have will be yours.

"And then there's Barrett and Company. I have expansion plans, sound ones. Next year, I intended to have you hire yourself an assistant. Now, with the baby, maybe we'll do it a little early. You can train the new person yourself and she—or he—can cover for you while you're out having the baby. In two years, we'll be ready to bring in another accountant, an all-around guy like me, but with a strong emphasis in tax accounting. That will free me up a little to court more large accounts.''

Andie watched his face. He looked so earnest now, as he talked about the future—a future he was offering to share with her. His generosity moved her deeply. She felt a kind of glowing warmth inside, a tenderness toward him, part admiration, part gratitude, part something she didn't dare give a name.

And within this special tenderness, the sadness remained. Clay had given up his best friend. And he was offering her half of all he had. All because she had been so very foolish and was determined now to raise the child she'd created.

Clay must have seen her remorse in her eyes. He misinterpreted it. ''Look. Andie. If you decide you don't want to work anymore, we'll manage. You'll be difficult to replace at the office, but I'd be willing to—''

She would burst into tears if he said one word more. She touched his lips. ''Stop. No more. Please.''

He wrapped his hand around hers and kissed the finger she'd used to shush him. ''What is it? What's the problem?''

''Quit talking. Listen.''

''All right. What?''

''I do *not* want to give up my job. I love my job.''

''All right. Fine. That's great with me.''

''I still hate that you've lost Jeff. I feel guilty about it. I'll probably always feel guilty about it.''

''Forget about Jeff.''

I will when you do, she thought. But there was no point in belaboring the issue anymore. ''All right.''

He still held her hand in his. He pressed it against his chest. She felt the beat of his heart. ''Marry me.''

''All right.''

He blinked. "I could have sworn you just said yes."

"I did."

"Are there any more *buts?*"

"No, there aren't."

He wrapped his free arm around her and pulled her close. "You won't regret it."

"I only hope *you* don't."

"I won't." He lifted her captured hand again and kissed her fingers once more. "I want to get going on this."

He sounded just the way he did at the office. The thought made her chuckle. "I imagine you have it all planned out."

"Yes."

"Well? Tell me."

"Tahoe or Reno. Right away, today. And then we'll rush back tomorrow night."

"Because of the work load at the office?"

"Exactly. But we'll have it taken care of. We'll be married, you know."

"Yes, Clay. I know." She thought of glow worms, suddenly. Glow worms and fireflies. That was how she felt right then, like some little creature that glows all by itself. Her mind was swimming.

Her own adopted cousin had turned out to be the man of her dreams. And now they would be married. Clay would be her husband. The doubts that still nagged at her seemed to mean nothing right then. Right then, she just felt wonderful, to think that she would sleep beside him every night. For the rest of their lives.

"And then, at the end of April, we could take a trip," Clay was saying. "By then, things will be quiet at the office and Dad can easily handle things alone. We'll go somewhere tropical, I think. Hawaii, maybe. For two weeks or so. We could spend a lot of time on a beach. And in bed ..."

Andie blushed. "I see."

"Well, then. What do you think?"

"I think yes. To all of it."

"Good. Tahoe or Reno?"

"I like Tahoe better."

"Tahoe it is." He was stroking her back. "We should call and get a hotel, shouldn't we?"

"I'm sure."

"And then maybe we should tell the folks."

She thought about the family. They wouldn't like finding out about the wedding after the fact. Her mother and her aunt wouldn't like it at all. On the other hand, if they were told now—

"What?" Clay prompted.

Andie pushed the image of her mother's disappointed face from her mind. "After we get back. We'll tell them then. If we tell them before—"

Suddenly, Clay caught on. "They'll want to come. You're right. It will slow us down."

She reached up and brushed his lips with her own. "Exactly."

He caressed the side of her face, toyed with the shape of her ear. "We should get a move on."

"Yes."

"There's only one problem."

"What?"

"I want to kiss you."

"You do?" Something funny happened in Andie's stomach.

"We only made love once last night. You were so tired."

She nodded. "I was. I conked out."

"But you don't seem tired now."

"Oh, I'm not. I'm not tired now at all."

"We could spare an hour, don't you think?" Clay's voice was low, hoarse. It made her stomach quiver all the more.

Andie pressed herself against him, feeling wild and wonderful—and feeling that way with *Clay,* of all people. It seemed so sinful, to feel wild and wonderful with Clay. So deliciously wicked. All those years he'd been her adversary. And now he was the object of her desire.

"Don't you think we could spare an hour?" Clay asked again.

Andie hastened to agree with him. "Oh, yes. An hour. Yes, definitely."

And then he kissed her.

Andie drank in the taste of him. He swept her mouth with his tongue as he had before. But now she brazenly returned the caress, meeting each hungry thrust with a parry of her own.

Clay's hands were on the tie at her neck again. He worked swiftly, and the wrinkled blouse slid to the floor. Then he unzipped her skirt and pushed it down.

Soon enough, she was naked, just as she'd been last night. Andie quivered as his hands roamed her bare flesh. And he went on kissing her. Would she ever get enough of those kisses of his?

She doubted it. This making love was a miracle to her. She'd waited so long to find out what it was all about.

There was a couch, in the family area beyond the kitchen and the breakfast table. Clay led her there. Or rather, they somehow ended up there, kissing and touching and moving across the floor at the same time.

He pushed her down on the couch and said he loved to look at her. And he *did* look at her. Andie was too dazed with desire to blush.

She wanted to see him, too, she realized. So she pulled at his clothes. At first, he tried to ignore her urging, caught up in his exploration of her as he was. But finally, he gave in. He stood and removed his jeans and his T-shirt, every last stitch, tossing them away as if he couldn't get free of them fast enough.

Andie sighed when she saw him, naked as she was at last. She smiled and held out her arms.

He needed no more encouragement. He came down to her. He kissed her breasts, suckling at them and teasing them lightly with his teeth, so that she wiggled and groaned and heard herself crying, "Yes..."

And then he kissed her belly and stroked it with his hand as well. She reveled in that. It felt so good, so warm and good.

And then he kissed her lower still. She gasped a little, when he parted her, right there on that couch in the dazzling light of day. But she didn't protest. How could she protest such wonder, such searing, glorious pleasure?

His tongue was there, tasting her. She moved against it, tossing her head on the throw pillows.

Her climax was swift and all-encompassing. And as soon as it took her, he rose above her, sliding into her with no other prelude, so that one minute she was empty and the next she was filled.

It seemed she reached consummation again then, immediately, as he moved in and out of her, slowly and deliberately, gentle yet demanding, just like the night before. She held on to him, raising herself to him, offering all that she was.

It went on and on. As before, it was so marvelous. How had she lived so long without this? She didn't know.

When his own culmination came, Andie was right there with him, falling off the edge of the universe all over again. They cried out at the same time.

Then they rested, all tangled up on the couch together, so that it was hard to tell where her body ended and his began.

Lying there, her neck a little cramped and her left leg asleep, Andie felt absolutely marvelous. She stroked Clay's shoulders and back with the hand he wasn't lying on. His skin was moist. As it began to cool, she felt the goose bumps break out on him. Or was it on her?

He murmured, "It's too cold to lie here naked. Come on." He rose, reaching for her hand. She stared up at him, thinking how great it was just to look at him. "Don't look at me like that," he commanded, "or we'll never get to Tahoe."

They showered together, probably an error in judgment as it led to more lovemaking—and a later start. When they were finally dressed, Clay made some calls and managed to get them a nice room in a good hotel-casino. And then he threw a few things in a bag.

Next, they went to Andie's so she could pack.

Andie had barely spread her suitcase open on the bed in her room when the phone rang. Clay ordered her not to answer it, but she did, anyway.

"Well, there you are," groused Ruth Ann. "I called twice last night. I was getting worried."

Clay was frowning at her. "Who is it?"

Andie whispered, "Ruth Ann." Clay rolled his eyes.

"Hey? You still there?" Ruth Ann demanded.

Andie spoke into the phone. "I'm here."

Ruth Ann grunted. "And where were you last night?"

"I was . . . busy."

"Gotcha. But that wasn't the question."

Andie muttered her friend's name warningly.

Ruth Ann, as usual, refused to take the hint. "What were you *busy* doing?"

Andie cast about for a good answer. But she took too long.

"Oh, sweet Saint Christopher," Ruth Ann declared. "I know. I can smell it. You've been with Clay."

"Look, Ruth Ann—"

"He's there now, right?"

"Ruth Ann, I—"

"Right?"

"Oh, all right. Yes."

Clay mouthed "Hurry up" at her. Andie signaled she was doing her best. Clay shook his head and then left the room.

Ruth Ann demanded, "It was great, wasn't it?"

Andie sank to the side of the bed. "Is nothing private in this world?"

"Not with me around. Well. Wasn't it?"

"Ruthie."

"Well?"

Andie couldn't suppress a giggle. "Yes."

Ruth Ann made a crowing sound. "I knew it, I knew it. Are you going to marry him?"

"Yes."

"Saint Francis! When?"

"Today."

"Hooray! Although I suppose this means I'm going to have to kiss off my dearest dream."

"What dream is that?"

"Being your matron of honor, you dolt."

"Oh. Right. Sorry."

"But it's okay. The dress always costs an arm and a leg, anyway. I'll save some bucks. I've got two sets of braces to pay for, after all."

"How sensitively put."

"Want me to be there?"

"I do..."

"But then again, you don't. Hey. It's okay. This is a special situation, I know. Where are you going?"

Andie gave her the phone number of their hotel in Tahoe. "We haven't told the folks yet."

"I understand."

"If they get worried and call you, just give them that number. Okay?"

"You bet. And wait. One more thing."

"What?"

"Does he know? Did you tell him about you know who?"

"I didn't have to tell him."

"Huh?"

"He already knew."

Ruth Ann was calling on more saints as Andie hung up the phone.

"What did you tell her?"

Andie looked up to find Clay standing in the doorway. She gave a rueful shrug. "Not much. Most of it she figured out on her own. She knows we're getting married today. And I gave her a phone number. In case our folks call her."

"That's fine." His look said he wanted to say more.

"What? What is it?"

"She knows. About Jeff?"

"Yes. But she'll never tell anyone."

Clay made a low sound—part groan, part sigh. "I know. I grew up with Ruth Ann, too, after all. Remember that time your dad grounded you for a month for burning your report card?"

"I remember," Andie admitted with a sigh.

"You were so outraged at the unfairness of the punishment that you ran away."

"Yes, it's true. I did."

"Ruth Ann knew where you were."

"Yes, but I'd sworn her to secrecy. She never talked, did she?"

"No. Eventually, you came home on your own, as I remember it."

"You remember right. As I said, she never tells my secrets. And I never tell hers."

Clay was silent. Andie understood the silence when he finally spoke.

"When the baby's born, my name goes in the space where it says *father of child.*"

Andie swallowed. "Okay."

"Just so you know." Suddenly, his voice was brisk. "Now get packing, will you?"

"Yes, sir!"

Andie packed quickly. They were finally ready to leave around three. The ride to Tahoe was uneventful and they managed to get checked into their hotel by five that night.

Then they went looking for a license. In Douglas County, they discovered, the county clerk kept long hours for the sake of all the couples who wanted to get married the quick and easy way. By seven they had the license in hand.

After that, they did some talking. Arguing, actually. Clay wanted to get to a chapel right away. Andie wanted dinner. Finally, Clay gave in. They decided to go back to the hotel and enjoy the remains of their one evening away. They ate in the hotel's best restaurant.

Then they went to their room, since that was where they really wanted to be, anyway. Andie reached out her arms to Clay. Getting married was the last thing on her mind.

But the next morning, when Andie would have lazed in bed awhile, Clay was up and eager to find a chapel and say their vows. Andie groused a little. He told her they had to get the job done.

And then she laughed at him for being so serious and calling marrying her a "job." He glowered at her for a moment. And then he was laughing, too.

She loved the sound of his laughter. Generally, Clay was not a laughing man. She thought briefly, with that now-familiar stab of regret, of Jeff Kirkland. Jeff was the one who could make Clay laugh like that.

But now she, Andie, was making him laugh. The thought filled her with hope for the future. Maybe her doubts were groundless, after all.

Clay told her she looked misty-eyed.

Andie replied that she had a right to be misty-eyed. It was her wedding day.

"Fine. Be misty-eyed. And get in that shower. I've ordered room service. You've got an hour to eat and get ready. Then we're gone."

"An hour!" She gave a shriek of feminine outrage. "To get ready for my *wedding?*"

"All right, don't have a coronary. You can have an hour and a half."

They bought two plain gold bands right there in the chapel. The vows were quick and simple. Andie recited them with feeling, looking into Clay's eyes. Clay said his part in a firm voice. He promised to love, honor and cherish Andie. And he didn't even stumble over that forbidden word, *love.*

When they left the chapel, it was nearly noon. Andie was hungry.

"Hardly news," Clay remarked dryly, and then put his arm around her and kissed her right there on the sidewalk underneath a fir tree.

They found a coffee shop before they headed home. As soon as her stomach was full, Andie began to fret about the family.

"They're probably worried about us." Andie poured the last of her hot water over a soggy tea bag. "Now that I think about it, we really should have left a message, called one of them or something, don't you think?''

"And said what?''

She scrunched up her nose at him, since no immediate answer came to mind. If they'd told the truth, half the family would have followed them up here to witness the event. And if they'd lied, Andie would have felt like a louse.

"Andie, they probably don't even know we're gone. And we'll be home soon, long before they have a chance to start worrying.''

"I've got a great idea." Andie pressed on the tea bag with her spoon, to get whatever was left in it out. "Let's call them.''

"What?''

"Let's call them." She set the spoon aside and sipped the lukewarm brew. "We can call them from here. You call your folks and I'll call mine. Then by the time we get home, they'll already have been mad at us for not telling them and they'll be on to the good part.''

"The good part?" Clay looked doubtful.

Andie pushed her cup away. "You know, where they smile and exchange significant looks and say they're sure we'll be happy together. What they'll really be thinking, of course, is that it's about time. But they would never, ever say such a thing. Well, except for Granny Sid. She might say it.''

Clay chuckled. "Yeah. She just might.''

With her finger, Andie traced a jagged heart that someone had carved into the tabletop. "I love them. I really do.''

"Then why the long face?''

"Oh, I don't know.''

"Yes, you do.''

"Sometimes I just wonder, that's all.''

"What?''

"What it would be like not to have to worry how the family will take it every time I make a major step in my life." She gave a wry chuckle. "I used to try not to care what they thought, when we were kids."

"Did you ever."

"But trying not to care never really worked. In my heart, I still *did* care. And I'd feel awful when Mom looked bewildered at something I'd done and Dad shook his head and said he didn't know what to do with me. Then on top of feeling awful, I'd have to pretend it didn't matter to me at all. It just wasn't any fun, trying not to care. So I gave it up and just let myself feel wretched when they'd shake their heads over me."

"Hey." His voice was teasing.

She looked up from the raggedly carved heart. "What?"

"They're going to be happy that we're married. I know they are."

"Yes, but your mother and my mother are going to be hurt that we didn't tell them first. But you don't have to worry about that."

"Why not?"

"Because they're not going to be unhappy with you. You're only a man. How could you be expected to know that one way for a girl to really annoy her mother and her aunt is to get married without even telling them, without giving them any chance at all to make a big fuss over the arrangements? *I'm* the one who's supposed to know that."

Clay just stared at her, flummoxed. "Well, I'm sorry. I guess."

"Oh, how can you be sorry? It doesn't even make any sense to you."

"Well, that's true."

"So don't be sorry. *I'm* not even sorry. After all, I was the one who made the choice not to call them before we left.

And I did it knowing that Mom and Aunt Della would be peeved.''

"Well, if you don't want *me* to be sorry, and *you're* not sorry, either, then why are we talking about this?''

"Because I want to call them before we go home. And I want you to understand *why* I want to call them.''

"Well, I still don't understand that.''

"I know. So just let me do it, okay? Just... humor an emotional pregnant lady.''

"Okay. Fine. Do it.''

Andie looked down at the jagged heart again, considering. "Well, maybe calling them wouldn't be such a good idea, after all. Maybe it shows more consideration to tell them face-to-face.''

Clay dared to agree. "I think you're right there.''

"So, okay then, we'll go see them. Yours first and mine second as soon as we get home.''

"Sounds good.''

"Or maybe, we should see *mine* first...''

Clay groaned under his breath and suggested they ought to be on their way.

Thelma McCreary jumped up from her chair. "You're *what?* I don't believe it. Say it again.''

Andie gripped Clay's hand a little tighter. He gave her a reassuring squeeze. "We're married, Mom. We got married this morning in Tahoe.''

"You and *Clay?*''

Andie sighed and smiled. "Yes, Mom. Me and Clay.''

Tears rose in Thelma's brown eyes. "Oh, honey.'' And then she was reaching out.

Clay let go of Andie's hand so she could rise and be enfolded in her mother's arms. As Thelma hugged Andie and sniffled in her ear, Clay received similar treatment from Joe, though the hug was heartier and there were no tears.

"Well, this *is* good news," Joe announced, after everyone had switched places and Joe had hugged Andie while Thelma hugged Clay. "This is *wonderful* news. Thelma, get out that bottle of champagne we've been saving and I'll—Thelma?"

Thelma choked back a sob, grabbed for a tissue from a side table nearby and blew her nose. "Yes, Joe. All right."

"Thelma, what in the world is the matter?"

"My baby. Married at last."

"Yes, well," Joe blustered, "it's about time, now, isn't it?"

Clay looked at Andie and both of them tried not to laugh. "It's about time" was Granny Sid's line, after all.

"Oh, it's wonderful. It truly is." Thelma dabbed her eyes again. "Have you told Della and Don?"

"Not yet." Clay shot another glance at Andie, a weary one. In the car, she'd changed her mind five times about whom they'd tell first. "We'll do that next."

"Well, I suppose you want to get right over there," Joe said. "But we've got time for a toast, don't we?"

"Sure. Plenty of time."

"I'll get the champagne, then." Thelma bustled toward the kitchen. She turned in the arch to the dining room. "Andie, honey. Why don't you come and give me a hand?"

Andie, who'd just sat back down, rose again. She knew what was coming when her mother got her alone. She tried not to sound grim. "All right, Mom."

In the kitchen, Andie stood on a stool to bring down the crystal flute glasses from their high cupboard. She included a glass for herself to be sociable, though she knew she wouldn't actually drink any of the champagne.

"Will you rinse and wipe them, please? It's been a while since we've had champagne."

"Sure." Andie took the glasses to the sink and set about cleaning them up.

Her mother produced a bottle of champagne from somewhere in the depths of her refrigerator. "I suppose I might as well open it. Your father's too rambunctious about it. Last time the cork hit my favorite lamp and blew a hole in the shade."

"Uh-huh." Andie set the last glass to drain and reached for the towel. Out of the corner of her eye, she saw her mother sink to a chair. She turned. "All right. Say it."

Thelma waved at the air in front of her face with the hand that wasn't clutching the champagne. "Oh, it's nothing. Nothing. I'm so happy for you."

"Look, Mom. Just say it, okay?"

"Well."

"Go on."

"I know it's selfish."

"I'm listening."

"You're my only child."

"That's true."

"And, well, it would have been nice to have been there, that's all. It would have been nice to have been included."

"You're mad at me."

"No, not mad. Hurt. A little. I'm sure Della will feel the same."

"Mom. When we made the decision, we didn't want to wait, you know? With the situation the way it is, with the baby and all."

Her mother gave a delicate little cough. "Yes. Of course, you're right, honey. I'm being selfish. I said I knew I was. But you're still my only child, as Clay is Della's. And now the only wedding we ever might have planned has already taken place."

"So then, you not only wanted to *be* there, you wanted to plan it all."

"Well, yes. Yes, I did. What's wrong with that?"

"There's nothing wrong with that, Mom. It just didn't turn out that way."

"It will take me a while to reconcile myself with this."

"I know, Mom."

"I think you should hug me and tell me how much you love me."

Andie took the champagne bottle from her mother's hand and set it on the floor. Then, kneeling, she wrapped her arms around her mother.

"I love you, Mom."

Her mother held her close and sobbed, "I love you, too. And I'm happy, really. Very happy."

"I'm glad."

"What's the holdup in there?" Andie's father called from the other room.

Thelma yanked out a counter drawer beside her and found a tissue. She blew her nose. "Woman talk! We're coming!" Then she looked at her daughter again. "What about you? Are *you* happy?"

Andie nodded.

"I'm glad. That *is* what really counts." Thelma dried her eyes. "Della will sulk, too, you know."

"I know."

"Want me to call her?"

"No way. She doesn't get to plan the wedding. She should at least get to tell me how much my lack of consideration has injured her."

At last, Thelma smiled. "Every year you become more understanding of your elders—did you know that?"

"It's called growing up, Mom."

"Whatever. It's lovely to see." Thelma picked up the champagne bottle and stood. "Now, let's get the cork out of this thing and get back in there before Clay and your father come looking for us."

"Good idea." Andie grabbed the towel and began polishing the glasses.

"Honey?"

"Um?"

"Clay is a good man."

"I know."

"I think things will be good, for both of you, now you've worked out whatever was . . . holding you back."

"So do I, Mom."

"And maybe I'm old-fashioned, but I think it's important for a child to have both of its parents, and for the parents to be husband and wife."

"I know you do, Mom."

"Honey . . ."

"What?"

"Oh, never mind. Just don't forget that I love you and you can talk to me."

"I won't. And thank you."

"I'm coming in there!" Joe called.

"Don't you dare! We'll be right there!" Thelma popped the champagne cork. It flew up in the air and made a dent in the ceiling. She wrinkled her nose at her daughter. "He'll never notice it, if you don't say anything."

Andie hung up the towel. "I promise, Mom. Not a word. Ever."

Chapter Ten

Andie awoke to the sound of thunder. Outside, she could hear the heavy pounding of rain. It pattered on the deck and beat on the roof before it tumbled down the gutters to the ground below. She looked at the clock: past two. She was alone in the bed.

There was a frigid draft coming from somewhere. She shivered and saw that the glass door to the deck was open a crack. Her robe was thrown across the chair by her side of the bed. She reached for it and wrapped it around herself. Then she rose and padded across the hardwood floor to the glass door.

She looked outside, scanning the deck for Clay as she started to push the door closed. Lightning streaked across the sky. She saw him, as the thunder boomed.

He stood at the railing, his body held very erect, his face tipped up to the pouring rain. He was naked. The rain streamed down his face, slicked his hair to his scalp and ran down his body in a thousand tiny rivulets. His face, in profile, was transfixed, pure, strong, very male.

Andie gasped. He took her breath away. She'd known him for nearly twenty years. But did she really know him at all? All those years she had taunted him for lacking a spirit of adventure, for being Cautious Clay.

And all this time, he'd been someone who stood naked in freezing rainstorms. It was humbling, she realized. How little we know of those who fill our lives.

As she watched, he turned his head slowly to meet her eyes through the glass of the door. It was as if he had felt the intensity of her gaze. Water ran in his eyes now and dripped off his chin and nose. He stared at her over his shoulder, his eyes far away, defiant. Lightning flashed and thunder cracked once again. And then he turned fully toward her and walked to where she waited beyond the glass door.

She pulled it open enough that he could step through and then closed it behind him to keep out the rain and the biting wind.

She could feel the coldness, the wetness of him as she turned from the door to face him. "What were you doing out there?" There was nothing of the worried wife in her voice, only her curiosity, her wonderment.

He shrugged. "I've always loved storms. My mother— not Della, the other one, Rita—she loved storms."

Andie opened her robe. "You're cold. Come here."

He took one step. She enfolded him, wrapping her robe and her arms around him. He sighed and she gasped as his body met hers. He was cold, so cold. She shivered as she gave him her body's heat.

He started kissing her before she had warmed them both. And then she forgot her shivering. He stepped back and scooped her against his chest and carried her to the bed.

They had been married a week. To Andie, it seemed that what they shared now had always been. He touched her and found her ready. He slid inside. Andie welcomed him with a lifting of her hips and a gratified sigh.

After their pleasure had crested and receded, she pulled the blankets up to shelter them.

"What was she like, your natural mother?"

He turned her and wrapped himself around her back, spoon fashion. Andie thought he wasn't going to answer her, but then he said, "She was a dreamy kind of person. It seemed to me like she was always off in her own world somewhere. I guess that's not surprising. For her, the real world wasn't too great. She was sick a lot. And she had trouble holding a job."

"Did you feel that she loved you?"

"Yes," he said after a moment. "I think she loved me. And she did the best she could."

"You never knew your father, right?"

"Don Barrett is my father." His voice was flat.

"I meant your natural father."

"I know what you meant. And you're right. I never knew him. I never even knew who he was. He was gone long before I was born."

"Do you ever wonder about him?"

"No."

She wanted to see Clay, so she rolled over and lifted up on an elbow. His face was in shadow. She thought of switching on the light but didn't. There was something safe and intimate about the dark. Maybe in the dark he would confide in her a little.

"What is it?" His voice was guarded.

"I just can't believe that you never wonder what he was like."

"I did wonder. When I was a kid. But I got over it."

"It just seems to me like something you would always wonder about."

"That's probably because *you* would always wonder, if you were me."

"That's true."

"But you're *not* me, Andie."

"Well, I know that. Whew. Do I ever."

He chuckled then and seemed to relax a little. He even took her hand and caressed it thoughtfully, toying with the gold bracelet of linked hearts she wore. "Look. Don and Della are all the parents I'll ever need. That is honestly and truly the way I feel."

"Do you hate your natural father?"

Clay sighed and stopped stroking her hand. "No, Andie. I don't hate him."

"There are agencies, aren't there, who will track down birth parents?"

"Yes, there are. And a lot of them operate using illegal means. They break confidentiality laws right and left."

"Yes, but—"

"Stop. Listen. I happen to believe that this country's adoption laws are humane laws, in most cases. I know there are people obsessed with finding kids or parents they lost. But I'm not one of them. I'm honestly not. So get that idea out of your head."

"What idea?" She tried not to sound guilty.

"I know you, Andie."

"What is that supposed to mean?"

"It means if you get it in your head to track down my birth father, you'll be doing it for *yourself,* not for me. The man is a complete stranger to me. I don't have any desire to meet a stranger who says he's my father."

"But it's natural, isn't it, to want to know where you came from?"

"For some people, I'm sure it is. For me, it's a moot point. I needed to *belong,* to be included in a real family. I wanted a true home, a place where they would always take me in if I needed them, no matter what. And I got what I needed when your aunt and uncle adopted me."

Andie leaned closer to him, trying to see what was really in his eyes. "Are you sure?"

"I am positive."

She plopped back onto her pillow and stared up at the shadowed ceiling. "I believe you."

He grunted. "You sound so disappointed."

She pulled the covers up around her chin again and rubbed her toe along Clay's leg. During the past week she'd discovered that one of the loveliest things about married life was the feel of Clay beside her in their bed.

He moved his leg toward her, a silent reply to her caressing toe. "Well? *Are* you?"

"What?"

"Disappointed."

She confessed, "I am, I guess. A little."

"Why?"

"Oh, I suppose it just occurred to me, right now while we were talking, that I could do this wonderful thing for you, find your *father* for you. It was going to be terrific. You were going to be so grateful. You'd never again bark at me at work because you couldn't find some file you needed. And at home, you'd look at me with adoration, because I'd reunited you with your past."

"I already look at you with adoration."

But not with love, she thought, before she could stop herself. She pushed the thought away, turned toward him and snuggled up close. "Good. Keep it up."

"I aim to please."

* * *

Ruth Ann demanded, "You're going to have to go into more detail about this. I don't get what you're saying."

It was Sunday afternoon. They were in the living room of Andie's apartment, packing books and knickknacks to take to the house on Wildriver Road. Andie had put off the job of closing up the place longer than she should have. Now the month was almost over and she had to be out in three days. As they packed, they'd been talking. And now Andie was trying to define her vague worries about her relationship with Clay.

"It's hard to explain. It's all so new between us."

"So try, anyway."

Andie scooped up another handful of books and stacked them in a box.

Ruth Ann, as usual, would not be evaded. "I said, try anyway."

"Oh, Ruthie..."

"Come on."

"Well, he's got this thing."

"What thing?"

"About love."

"What about love?"

"He doesn't believe in it, not in man-woman love, anyway."

Ruth Ann reached a top shelf and took down more books. She handed them to Andie. "Explain."

Andie bent to put the books in the box with the others. "He believes in the love you have in families, you know, the urge to care for each other and help each other in life. But he doesn't believe in being *in* love. He says that's only sex."

Ruth Ann leaned on the bookcase and let out a disgusted groan. "Men."

"So even if he ever got to the point where he might be in love with me, he's not going to be in love with me, because he doesn't believe in it. You know?"

"Blessed Saint Anselm, my head is spinning."

"And I want his love."

"Not unreasonable. Do you love him, er, I mean, are you *in love* with him?"

Andie turned her attention to a pair of carved mahogany bookends that her father had bought her two birthdays ago. She began carefully wrapping them in tissue.

"Well. Are you?"

"It's too soon to tell."

Ruth Ann collected another stack of books. "You want my advice?"

"Yeah. I suppose."

Since Andie was still busy with the bookends, Ruth Ann climbed off her chair and boxed the handful of books herself. "Come on. Fake some enthusiasm, or I won't tell you what I think."

"All right. I do. I want your advice."

"He's acting like a man. But *you're* acting like a woman. I don't know which is worse."

"What's that supposed to mean?"

"It means that until you're at least sure you're *in love* with him, why borrow trouble? Are you having the best time of your life or what?"

"Yes. Yes, I am."

"Then cheer up." Ruth Ann climbed up on the chair again. "There'll be plenty of time to suffer if things ever really go wrong."

Just then, the door burst open.

"Hey, Mommy. Lookit this." A big brown box with two little sneaker-clad feet sticking out from under it staggered into the living room. "I'm a box. Pack me." The box fell over, giggling hysterically.

Ruth Ann rolled her eyes and grabbed another handful of books as her younger son, Kyle, wriggled his way out of the box.

Clay came in then, carrying a stack of boxes. Andie got up and went to meet him. "Hello, there."

He returned her smile. "Hiya." They kissed around the stack of boxes.

Behind them, Ruth Ann made some knowing remark about newlyweds.

Andie asked, "How'd you guys do?"

Clay set the boxes down on the table in the little dining nook right off the living room. "Not bad for a Sunday. We hit the jackpot at Grocery Superstop."

"Yeah, did we ever," Kyle put in. "We had so many boxes, I had to ride with one on my head the whole way home. It was really funny, wasn't it, Clay?"

Clay smiled at the boy. "A riot. Come on. Help me get the rest from the car."

"You bet." Swaggering just a little with the importance of this grown-up job he was doing, Kyle followed Clay out.

"Clay's good with kids," Ruth Ann said when the boy and the man were gone. "Kyle was really irked this morning when he heard he was going with me instead of to the batting cages with Johnny and Butch." Butch was Ruth Ann and Johnny's older boy. "Kyle hates to be stuck with the women. I was sure I was going to have nothing but trouble from him all day."

Andie chuckled. "I'll bet. But the minute he saw Clay he perked right up."

"Exactly. And now he's just thrilled to be driving from one store Dumpster to another, scavenging for packing boxes."

"Yeah, it worked out fine."

Ruth Ann suddenly looked reproachful. "Clay's going to be great with the baby, Andie."

"I know that."

"And you're nuts about him, even if you're not willing to admit it's love yet."

"I know. And stop looking at me like that."

"You should get down on your knees every day, I'm telling you, and thank the good Lord."

Andie met her friend's gaze. "I do, Ruthie. Believe me. I do."

"So do what I told you. Stop worrying. Let yourself be happy."

"I'll do my best, Ruthie. I swear I will."

Over the next few months, Andie took her friend's advice seriously. She stopped borrowing trouble, stopped worrying that Clay's heart would forever be closed to her. Instead, she concentrated on making a good life with him.

And it worked. Life was good. She and Clay put in killing hours at the office through the first half of April and didn't mind them a bit. After all, when they went home, they had each other.

Then the office settled down. Uncle Don took over while Andie and Clay went to Hawaii for the honeymoon they hadn't had time for until then. For nine whole days, they did nothing but bask in the sun, swim in the surf, eat, sleep and make love. After the lovemaking, Clay would often lie with his head against the new roundness of Andie's belly and tell her that he could feel the baby move.

She laughed. "But it's only like moth wings, even to me."

"I can feel it," he assured her. "There. There it is."

When they returned, they signed up for natural childbirth lessons. Clay was eager to be her birthing coach. He went with her to her obstetrician and asked more questions than she ever would have thought of. And then, the next Saturday, he drove her down to Sacramento to one of the huge superbookstores there. He bought out what seemed like half the section on pregnancy and childbirth.

And then at home, while Andie planned how she'd make the small bedroom next to theirs over for the baby, Clay pored over all the baby books he'd bought.

"This is fascinating," he told her. "You should read this. It tells about the baby's development inside the womb, week by week."

Andie was trying to choose curtains. "Just read me the good parts," she suggested vaguely.

He took her at her word. "Let's see. We're at eighteen weeks. Right about now, the baby has eyebrows, hair on its head and lanugo. That's fine hair all over the body. This lanugo may help in temperature regulation, or it may be an anchor for the vernix caseosa, which is a waxlike substance that protects the baby from immersion in the amniotic fluid."

"How charming," Andie remarked with a shudder.

"It's a miracle," Clay said with such a great show of solemnity that she knew he was at least partially teasing her.

She pointed at a crib set in one of her catalogs. "What about these?"

"Too froufrou."

"What does that mean?"

"It means that I really hate ruffles. A kid could suffocate in all those ruffles."

"Okay, how about these?"

"Better. Much better."

A week later, he read her some more. "Okay, nineteen weeks. 'First sucking motions likely. Can grip with hands. The ability to blink develops, though the eyelids are still fused...'"

And then the week after that: "'Twenty weeks. The baby's about ten inches long. Eight to nine ounces in weight...'"

Andie got to where she'd groan a little when he brought out his favorite book and opened it to the page that described the baby's current development. But it was a happy groan. It was wonderful to see him so involved, to really start to believe in the amazing thing that had happened: the baby she'd been sure she was going to be raising alone had a father after all.

At the end of May, they hired another secretary at the office. Her name was Linda Parks. She was a single mother, in her forties and in need of a dependable job with good benefits. She was also a crack typist and knew both the spreadsheet and word processing programs that Barrett & Co. used. Linda had worked in another accounting firm in Oakland, from which she came highly recommended. She'd moved to the foothills seeking a safer environment for her children.

Linda learned quickly. By the middle of June, since business was only moderate, Andie was able to leave Linda on her own at the office for several hours a day. Clay kept busy, even though it wasn't nearly the rat race at work that it had been at the beginning of the year.

He did the social scene more, took clients to lunch and played golf. When Andie kidded him about partying on company time, he reminded her that the only way to build the client base was to do a little wining and dining. She laughed and said she knew that very well. Couldn't he stand a little teasing? He gave up looking wounded and admitted that he supposed he could.

June became July. In her seventh month, Andie grew ripe and round as a peach.

Clay went on reading about the baby's growth.

"'Week twenty-six. The baby's eyelids can open and close. Increased muscle tone. Sucking and swallowing skills continue to develop...'"

The baby's room was all ready. The curtains and all the bedding were yellow, with little bears and balloons on the wallpaper. The crib, bureau and changing table had been Andie's when she was a baby. They'd been stored in the attic at her mother's. Somehow, over the years, the wood had become worn and scratched. Clay refinished the furniture himself, insisting that Andie stay well away from the fumes of the stripping compound.

He continued with the progress reports.

"'Huge changes taking place in the nervous system. The brain grows greatly during this month. Some experts believe this is the beginning of true consciousness...'"

In mid-July, Andie and Clay began their childbirth classes. Once a week, they went to a room at the public library and joined six other couples learning relaxation techniques, practicing breathing, seeing graphic films of real births.

At home, Clay read, "'By twenty-eight weeks, all the baby's senses are in working order...'"

Clay talked to the baby all the time. Sometimes he called it "he," sometimes "she." Andie asked him which he'd prefer. He said he didn't care. She knew he told the truth.

He read on. "Conscious relaxation, deep breathing and meditative states in the mother stimulate the baby's entire body and developing mind. Music and gentle, repetitive sounds are good for the baby's hearing. When the mother sunbathes, gets massaged, swims, walks, or even showers, the baby's touch perception and balance are improved."

By August, Andie was becoming increasingly uncomfortable. To her it seemed she lumbered around like an elephant, though her weight was in the average range for a woman in her eighth month. She felt hot all the time, too. And everything she ate seemed to hover somewhere up around her breastbone. And she dreamed of the night she'd be able to lie on her back without feeling dizzy—or on her stomach without feeling giddily numb, as if she were trying to rest on a basketball.

Clay's response to her complaints was to read to her from his library of baby books, explaining that she couldn't lie on her back because it pressed on the vena cava, a major vein. And her stomach now literally *was* shoved up between her lungs, so it made sense that food felt as if it got stuck there. And the reason she felt hot all the time was because her heart had expanded in size and her capillary action was greatly increased.

Andie groaned and threw a pillow at him. She had lots of pillows. She had to arrange them strategically under various parts of herself at night so she could sleep. It was getting to the point that she wasn't even interested in making love anymore, which would have seemed impossible just a few weeks before.

Clay, through it all, was patient and wonderful. She *despised* him for being so terrific. Almost as much as she loved him.

And she did love him, was *in love* with him. Sometime in the past few months, she'd accepted the reality of her love and welcomed it. It didn't even seem to matter anymore that Clay still clung to his frustrating belief that the kind of love Andie knew she felt for him didn't exist.

Probably part of the reason it didn't matter was that she knew he loved her, too. In exactly the same way that she loved him, even if he wouldn't admit to it.

Finally, she told him of her love.

It was a night in the fourth week of August. Andie hadn't been able to sleep. So Clay was rubbing her neck and shoulders, reminding her to breathe slowly and evenly, to picture fields of flowers, to see the color blue.

She thought the words of love and they rose to her lips. She released them.

"I love you, Clay."

He went on working his soothing magic with his hands. "Did you hear what I said?"

"I heard. Breathe slowly. In and out."

"I'm *in love* with you."

"Relax."

"I mean it."

"Whatever. Keep breathing."

She turned around so she could look at him. The room was dark. It was hard to see his expression. She switched on the bedside lamp.

"I love you."

Something happened in his face. Something tormented yet hopeful, a passionate expression, swiftly quelled. The look was there and gone so fast that the minute it disappeared, Andie wondered if she had really seen it.

Was it possible that he *wanted* to believe her and didn't dare? Or was her heart making her see things that weren't there? Whatever the truth was, the mysterious expression was long gone. Now he merely looked puzzled and a little concerned.

He lifted a bronze eyebrow. "Do you want me to say I love you, too? Is that it?"

The lifted eyebrow did it. Suddenly, she thought of Mr. Spock of "Star Trek" fame. As Spock would say, "But, Captain, love is illogical..."

Andie burst out laughing.

Clay continued to look perplexed and perhaps a bit pained. "Are you all right?"

"I'm fine." She fell over sideways on the bed, holding her huge middle, still giggling.

"Andie..."

"Never mind." Somehow she collected herself. And then she sat up again and showed her back to him, turning her head so she could smile at him, smoothing her mass of hair out of his way over her shoulder. "Would you rub my neck a little more? It really does feel wonderful."

He looked at her with equal parts wariness and suspicion. And then he shook his head. She thought he muttered something about women under his breath. But then he turned off the light and put his incredible hands to work once more.

Andie sighed; it felt so good. She breathed evenly as he had instructed her to do.

And she smiled to herself, marveling at how downright pigheaded her husband could be. She pondered the idea that she was probably going to live a whole lifetime at his side, during which he would never once utter those three incredible little words.

But she was also thinking that it was okay. She could live without those words. Because she knew, even though Clay refused to give his love a name, that he did love her—was *in love* with her. Clay showed his love every day in ten thousand little ways. It was enough.

Clay's hands strayed. They glided, warm and soothing, over her shoulders and down her arms. "Feel sleepy now?"

"Um..."

He scooted up close behind her and put his arms around her. Then he gently explored her belly. After a few moments, his hands went still. "There. A foot, I think."

She investigated where he was touching. "No." She leaned fully against him, resting her head in the crook of his shoulder, feeling sheltered and protected as she'd never dreamed she would be. "That was an elbow, no doubt about it."

He chuckled. And then he nuzzled her hair aside and kissed her earlobe. "You're so beautiful, Andie."

"There's so much of me. It had better be beautiful."

"I'm not kidding."

"Neither am I. Do you realize that my belly button is an *outie* now? Sometimes it actually shows through my clothes. It's gross."

"You're beautiful."

"You're overworked and losing your mind."

"What we have—it's very good."

A warmth spread through her. This was as close as he would come, she knew, to speaking of his love. "Yes, Clay. It is. It's the absolute best."

Carefully he turned her so that she lay back in his arms. He supported her with his arm and his thigh so that that major vein he'd told her about wasn't put under pressure. And then he kissed her, a very slow kiss.

When he lifted his head, Andie decided that maybe she still liked sex, after all. His hand strayed, caressing, stroking. Andie sighed. For a magical half hour, she forgot everything but the touch of those hands.

When at last he helped her arrange her pillows, she was truly ready for sleep.

"Clay?"

"Yeah?"

"Thanks, Clay."

"For what?"

"For all of it. For our lives together. For being you."

"You're welcome. Go to sleep."

Smiling, Andie closed her eyes.

The next morning, Madeline Kirkland called.

Chapter Eleven

They were sitting at the breakfast table. They'd already eaten and Clay was having one last cup of coffee while Andie nursed her peppermint tea. It was a beautiful day, especially now, in the morning, with the air just a tad breezy and the windows open. Later, Andie would close up the house and turn on the air conditioner to fight the fierce heat of the afternoon. But just now, it was lovely.

Andie was planning to stay home all day. At the office now, Linda was managing fine. So Andie had decided to start taking it easier, with the baby due in a month. She had slashed her own hours to twenty a week. It was working out quite well.

"More coffee?" Andie asked.

Clay rustled his paper and grunted. Andie lumbered to her feet and shuffled over to the sink, thinking wryly of beached whales, of grounded hippos, cursing the power of gravity and swearing she wouldn't let it get her down.

The phone rang just as she stuck her mug of water in the microwave to heat. The phone was on the wall, not far from where Clay sat. But he was absorbed in his paper.

Andie waddled on over there and picked it up. "Hello?"

A silence, then a strange woman's voice. "Oh. Hello." The voice hesitated. "Is this Clay Barrett's house?"

Andie smiled. An old girlfriend of Clay's, she thought, someone he hadn't seen in a while who didn't know he'd been married. "Yes, it is."

The woman took in a breath. "Well, I..." The voice trailed off. "I wonder if..." Andie began to think the woman sounded troubled, or under some sort of strain. "Please. This is Madeline Kirkland. I need to... May I speak with Clay?"

As soon as Andie heard the name, she felt dizzy. She gripped the section of kitchen counter right beside her to steady herself. Madeline Kirkland, Jeff's wife. What could she want? What possible reason could she have for calling Clay?

The worst came immediately to mind: that Madeline had somehow found out about the baby.

"Hello, are you there?"

Andie forced herself to speak. "Yes. Of course. Just a minute." She put her hand over the receiver.

Clay had already lowered his paper. He was looking at her, alarmed by what he saw. "Andie, what—?"

"Madeline," she said. "Madeline Kirkland." She held the phone close to her heavy belly, not extending it, almost hoping he'd refuse to take the call.

Clay looked at the receiver, his thought the same as Andie's.

He didn't want to take it. He wanted to shake his head and walk out of the room. If it had been Jeff, he would have.

But it wasn't Jeff. It was Madeline. Innocent Madeline. Clay thought the world of Madeline.

He stood. Andie put the phone in his hand.

"Sit down," he said quietly to his pale wife, before he spoke into the receiver. "Hello, Madeline."

"Clay? Oh, Clay..."

"What is it?"

"Clay, you've been a stranger." Her voice sounded so odd, fiercely controlled yet edged with frenzy. He was positive that somehow she had found out the truth about Jeff and Andie and the baby. "We've missed you, Clay. Very much."

"Well, I..." What the hell could he say? "I've been busy. Really busy. I, um, got married."

"Oh, Clay. You did? Was that her? Did she answer the phone?"

"Yes. I'm sure I've mentioned her. My cousin by adoption. Andie."

"Oh. Yes, I remember. Andie was the one you used to always fight with when you were kids, right?"

"Yes, that's the one."

"Well. Congratulations."

"Thank you."

There was an absolutely deadly pause. Andie was staring at him, agony in her eyes. And he still had no clue what was going on with Madeline.

Madeline said, "Oh, Clay. I don't know how..." And then her voice closed off. She made a painful, choking sound, then managed to control herself. "My mother was going to do this. But I... I thought it would help me. To hear your voice. Jeff loved you so."

Loved. Past tense. "Madeline?"

"Oh, I'm making a mess of this."

"Of what?"

"Of telling you."

"Telling me what?"

"About Jeff. Oh, Clay. He... Jeff died, Clay. Yesterday."

Clay sank to his chair, not even realizing he was sitting down until he was already there.

In his ear, tight and frantic, Madeline kept on. "He bought this new sports car. It was beautiful. But you know Jeff. A new toy. He played...he played too hard with it. He went too fast."

"Too fast?"

"Yes. Down Mulholland. Like some crazy kid. You know Mulholland, don't you, Clay? All those turns. He..." A sound came from Madeline, a keening sound. It started out low and slid impossibly high. Clay waited, while she gathered her forces once more. "He went over the cliff. It was a vertical drop, about two hundred feet. He died instantly, they told me. He didn't suffer any pain."

Beside him, Andie spoke. She asked if he was okay. He waved her away. He couldn't deal with her now. There was a huge something, like a rock, inside his chest. He breathed around it. He did not let himself remember Jeff, on the beach that last time, his hands in his pockets, the gulls wheeling over head.

"All right, bud. I'm dead...."

"Clay?" Madeline said.

Clay closed his eyes and rubbed at the sockets, rubbed the memory away. He reminded himself that Madeline had just lost the man she'd loved all her life and that Madeline was the one to think about now.

"What can I do?" he asked.

"Oh, Clay..."

"What? Anything. Tell me."

"I knew you'd say that. Thank you."

"What?"

"Okay. Yes, I'll tell you. The funeral's the day after to-morrow. Saturday. At eleven in the morning. It would mean a lot to me if you'd be there."

He answered automatically. "Of course I will."

"And would you be a pallbearer?"

"Yes, certainly."

"Oh, that's good. It will be good. To see your face. To remember the good times."

"Yes. The good times."

"Do you want to stay at the house?"

His numbed mind tried to follow what she was asking him. "The house?"

"The new house. You were there, remember, that last time you dropped in, several months ago? When you and Jeff got mugged at the beach?"

"Oh. Yeah." So that was what Jeff had told her.

"I'm not staying there myself. I just can't, not now. I'm at my parents' house for a while. But if you'd like to—"

"No. Listen. I'll get a hotel room. It's no problem. Where is the funeral and what time do I need to be there?"

Beside him, Andie gasped. Clay realized he'd been do-ing his best to block her out of his mind. Now she'd heard the word *funeral* and was starting to put things together.

"Jeff? Is it Jeff?" Andie asked. Her eyes were two black smudges in her white, white face.

Clay nodded. Then he stood to take the pencil from the notepad that was hanging on the wall by the base of the phone. Madeline gave him the information he needed and he scribbled it down. Then he promised to be there tomor-row.

"I'll call you," he said, "as soon as I get there."

"You'll call me at my parents' house?" Madeline asked.

"Right. What's the number there?"

Madeline rattled off the number, then went on, "Yes, please call. I'd appreciate that. Things are crazy. I hope we can spend a little time together, but I don't know how things will go."

"I understand."

"It might not seem that I appreciate your being there. But I do. I really do. He loved you so. You're everything he ever wanted to be—did you know that?"

"No, I didn't."

"It's true. He used to tell me that. That he wished he could be like you. You always worked so hard, knew what you wanted and kept your goals in mind whatever you did. And with you, responsibility was like a sacred trust." Madeline gave a strangled little laugh. "That's how he said it, 'With Clay, responsibility is like a sacred trust.'"

"Look, Madeline, I—"

"I know, I know. I'm babbling. But I can't seem to help it. And I just want you to know these things. I want to say them now, when they're in my head and I have the chance. Because I'm grateful to you Clay, I really am."

"For what?"

"Oh, Clay. I know that whatever you said to him over the holidays last year, whatever happened then, it made all the difference. When he came back, he was changed. He really wanted to marry me then. Always before, there'd been something in him that held back. We had a marriage, we were *together,* for at least a little while. And a lot of that was because of you."

"I understand," Clay said again. What the hell else could he say to something like that?

"Well, I . . . thanks for listening." Madeline said.

"It's okay."

"I should go."

"Of course."

"But I'll see you tomorrow, or at the funeral."

"Yes. Whatever. You take care."

"I will. Goodbye."

The line went dead. Clay hung the receiver back on the wall.

"Clay?" Andie was looking up at him, her face a blank, her eyes haunted. "Oh, Clay. It's Jeff?"

"Yes."

"Dead?" She said the word on a whisper, as if she hardly dared utter it.

"Yes."

"When?"

"Yesterday. A car accident. He bought a new car and drove it too fast."

"Oh." Andie grimaced, touched her belly.

"What is it?"

"Nothing. The shock."

"Are you sure?"

"Positive." She put her hand against her mouth, shook her head. "Oh, I'm so sorry. It's so awful. That poor woman."

"Yes. She asked me to go to the funeral. I'm going, for her sake."

"Of course."

"I'll fly down tomorrow."

"Oh, Clay. Are you all right?" She reached for his hand. He moved just enough that she didn't connect. "I'm fine. Really." He looked at his watch. "I should get going."

She stared at him. "Where?"

"To work. I'll be late."

"Work? Now? Clay, I don't think—"

"I've really got to go."

"But—"

"Can you call and get me a flight? Tomorrow afternoon would be best. I could check in at the office in the morning, see that everything's under control and then fly out of Sacramento later in the day. Will you do that?"

"Of course, but don't you think that—?"

"If you can't get an afternoon flight, then do what you can. Morning, if you have to. Or night, if all else fails. And I'd like to return as early as possible Sunday."

"I understand. But, Clay—"

"And also, can you get me a reservation at a decent hotel in Brentwood or nearby? The funeral will be in Brentwood and I'd like to keep surface travel to a minimum. And I'll need a rental car."

"All right. I'll take care of it. But I—"

"I have to go, Andie. I have to get out of here."

"Clay, I really don't think you should drive right now."

"I'll be fine."

"Please, Clay. Stay home for a while. Just let yourself get adjusted to what's happened, before you get into a car." Her voice was reasonable, very controlled. But her eyes were pleading with him.

He understood that she was worried for him and that she probably didn't want to be alone. But he knew he could handle himself all right in a car. And as far as her needs, he just couldn't think about them at the moment. He didn't have anything to give her right now. He was empty inside, except for that huge, rocklike something that filled up his chest.

"I have to go." He moved swiftly, around the table and across the room to the hall. He went to the coat closet, grabbed his briefcase and jacket. Then he fled to the garage.

He flung open the door of the car, tossed his briefcase across the seat and jumped in. He'd backed out of the garage and sent the door rumbling down again with the aid of the automatic opener before he allowed himself to relax a fraction. By then, he was sure that Andie wasn't going to try to follow him.

* * *

In the house, Andie sat in the kitchen chair for several minutes before she did anything else. She practiced breathing slowly and evenly. She tried to absorb the enormity of what had just occurred.

Jeff Kirkland was dead. Clay's best friend, the biological father of her child, was gone for good and all.

It didn't seem possible. He was out of their lives, yes. They probably would never have seen him again, anyway. Yet Andie had always assumed he would go on living his own life down there in Los Angeles, married to a woman named Madeline.

But now, fate had played the cruelest of tricks. Now Jeff Kirkland wouldn't go on. And that seemed hideous to Andie. Hideous and wrong.

She couldn't stop thinking about Madeline. Madeline would have to go on. Andie had never even met Madeline. Yet she knew the kind of pain Madeline must be suffering. Madeline was near her own age, a young woman, newly married, just like herself. And now Madeline was a widow.

What would that be like, to be a widow? To live the rest of her life without Clay? Andie thought of sleeping in their bed alone, sitting here at the breakfast table every morning alone. Such thoughts brought with them an empty, vast kind of pain.

"Oh, Clay," she whispered to herself, picturing him barreling along Wildriver Road, attempting the impossible, trying to outrun the anguish of losing his best friend twice. "Be careful, my darling," she whispered fervently. "Keep yourself safe." She closed her eyes and sent a little prayer winging toward heaven, a prayer for his safety, and then another for Madeline, whom she didn't even know.

Andie felt her own guilt in this, the guilt that had always been there since her one foolish night with Jeff Kirkland.

What Clay would have to suffer now would be doubly hard because of what she herself had done.

Clay hated deceptions, yet he would go to Jeff's funeral and pretend, for Madeline's sake, that everything was as it had always been. That the dead man had never stopped being his friend.

All because Andie McCreary and Jeff Kirkland had behaved so irresponsibly last New Year's Eve.

Yet how could Andie totally regret her own thoughtless indiscretion? It had brought the baby, who, even now, unborn, seemed such an important and transformative part of her life. And, in a roundabout, crazy way, it had brought her the true love she'd given up on finding.

Sometimes she wondered if, without the baby, she and Clay would ever have found their way to each other. They had such a history of hostility. They had both been so careful, over the years, to shield themselves from any intimate contact with each other. It had taken something enormous, another life coming, to break through all the walls.

For the baby's sake, Clay had given himself permission to pursue her. And because of the baby, she had been vulnerable. The walls had come down.

Would Jeff's death raise the walls all over again?

Andie shook her head. She couldn't afford to think such a thing.

With a little sigh, she rose. There were dishes to put in the dishwasher. And maybe after that, she'd go upstairs and make the bed. Put a load of laundry in the washing machine, dust the glass tables in the living room.

And then, when she was reasonably sure she could talk without bursting into tears, she'd call a travel agent she knew in town and see about making the arrangements for the trip to Los Angeles.

* * *

After she made the arrangements, Andie called Clay at the office. Linda said he couldn't come on the line right then. He would get back to her.

Andie was so relieved to hear he was there and safe that she didn't worry too much about his refusal to come to the phone. But then, a few hours later, when she called again and got the same response from Linda, Andie began to believe that Clay was evading her.

But she didn't allow herself to stew about it. He was upset about Jeff. She understood that. And he needed time to accept what had happened. She didn't call him again.

Instead, she called Ruth Ann. Ruth Ann cried when Andie told her about Jeff's death.

"Blessed Mother Mary," Ruth Ann sobbed. "Why am I doing this? I loathed and despised that jerk for what he did to you."

"It's because you have a big heart, Ruthie. And because no man should die when he's young and strong and still has years of life ahead of him."

Ruth Ann sobbed some more and blew her nose. "That's right. That is so right." She sniffed. "How's Clay taking it?"

"Not well, so far. But it was only this morning that we heard."

"He needs time."

"I know."

"Listen, how about if I come over?"

"No, I'm fine. But thanks."

"You sure?"

"Yes."

"Well, you know I'm here. Just call. And I'll be there."

"I know, Ruthie. And it helps. It really does."

After that, Andie called her mother.

"Oh, Andie. Such a young man," Thelma said. "It's a tragedy."

"Yes."

"His poor parents. I think that would be the worst thing. To have a child die before you."

"I believe that both of his parents are dead, Mom."

"Oh. How sad. He seemed like a nice young man, too. I'm so sorry. How's Clay?"

"As well as can be expected. He's at work now."

"Will he be going to the funeral?"

"Yes. Jeff's wife, Madeline, asked him to be a pall-bearer."

"And of course he will."

"Yes."

"What about you?"

"Me?"

"Well, with the baby coming and all, I suppose it's wisest if you stay at home."

"No, I'm going." Andie came to the decision just as she said the words. "I don't want Clay to be alone."

Andie expected her mother to argue with her, to launch into all the reasons she should stay home and be careful of her unborn baby. But Thelma surprised her. Her voice was sad and accepting. "I know what you mean. If it were your father's friend . . . well, I do understand. And you're feeling all right, aren't you?"

"I'm feeling just fine, Mom."

"How long will you be down there?"

"We'll leave Friday and be back by Sunday afternoon." Andie gave her mother the phone number of the hotel. As soon as she hung up, Andie called the travel agent again and managed to add herself to all the reservations. After that, she went to see her doctor, who provided the release form that the travel agent had said she'd need in order to fly this late in her pregnancy.

Clay arrived home at 7:49. Andie forced herself not to run—or in her case, waddle—out to the garage the minute she heard the door rolling open. Instead, she calmly pulled his dinner from the oven where she'd been keeping it warm and set it on the table.

She heard the inside garage door open and close, his footsteps on the hardwood floor. She heard him stop at the coat closet, to get rid of his jacket and his briefcase. At last, he appeared.

"I stopped by Doolin's." Doolin's was a bar in town. "For a drink."

She gave him a warm smile and didn't mention that he'd never stopped by Doolin's before in the five months they'd been married. "I kept your dinner warm."

"I'll wash my hands."

Clay came to the table five minutes later. Andie sat opposite him, sipping a glass of milk as he doggedly ate.

"Did you make the plane reservations?"

"Yes."

"For what time?"

"Two in the afternoon tomorrow. Out of Sacramento, arriving at LAX at 3:10."

"That's perfect. What about the hotel?"

"The Casa de la Reina. Triple A gives it four stars. And it's about two miles from the church."

"That sounds fine. Thanks."

"You're welcome."

She waited quietly as he finished up the meal. He talked of the office, of how well Linda was doing, of a dispute with a new client, a big account that Clay had knocked himself out to acquire, but now was just about to kiss goodbye.

"He wants to make a lot of money, and then pay zero taxes. I told him I'm good, but I won't cheat for him. It went downhill from there."

Andie listened sympathetically and waited for him to talk about what was really on his mind: Jeff.

It never happened. The few hours until bedtime slipped by.

After he brushed his teeth, Clay left the bathroom while Andie was still washing her face. When she returned to the bedroom, the light was off and Clay was a motionless lump on his side of the bed.

Suppressing a sigh, Andie approached her own side. Once there, she positioned her nest of pillows and then carefully arranged herself so that her upper knee was supported and her stomach rested comfortably on a pillow of its own. Through this procedure, Clay, who usually made a big production of moving her pillows around for her until she had them just right, remained still as a stone.

Andie settled in. She closed her eyes. She told herself to be patient, to give him time.

Yet she couldn't resist asking hesitantly, "Clay, are you awake?"

No answer. But she could feel the tension coming from him. He was not asleep.

"Clay, don't you think we should talk?"

He stirred, rolled over and gently patted her shoulder. "Go to sleep, Andie. Don't worry. Everything will be fine."

And that was all. Andie felt miserable. She hardly slept the whole night.

The next morning was a replay of the night before. Clay was a thousand miles away from her, though he persisted in the fiction that everything was just fine. He rose and showered, shaved and dressed. He ate his breakfast, drank his coffee and then returned to the bedroom to pack his bag.

Then he told her, "I might as well go directly from the office to the airport, don't you think?"

She smiled patiently at him, though she was becoming angry in her heart. "They'll be dropping the tickets off here at the house, by express mail, around eleven."

"You should have had them sent to the office."

"Well, it's a little too late to change things now. But I'd be happy to drive them over."

"Were you planning to come in this afternoon?" Lately, she'd been working from one to five on Fridays. But she wouldn't today, of course, because she was going with Clay.

She shook her head. "Actually, today I was going to call Linda and see if everything seemed under control. If she didn't need me, I was going to stay home."

"Fine, then. I'll come back and get the tickets."

"You're sure?"

"Yes." He kissed her on the cheek, a chaste little peck that made her want to grab him and shake him and demand to know what he'd done with her husband. Because he wasn't her husband, not this cold, distant stranger who seemed to be in such a hurry to get away from her. "Goodbye, then. I'll see you when I come back for the tickets."

Andie opened her mouth to tell him that the tickets weren't the only thing he'd be picking up this afternoon; she was going, too. But somehow, all she said was "Goodbye, Clay."

She reasoned that if she told him now, there would only be a big argument. She would wait until he came back for the tickets to tell him. That would be soon enough for the confrontation.

The minute he was gone, she went in the bedroom to pack her own bag.

"Absolutely not." Clay glared at her. "You are not coming with me."

"Yes, I am, Clay." They were standing in the little service porch area that led out to the garage. Andie's suitcase was at her feet.

"It's not safe for the baby."

"I'm nearly a month from my due date. I've had a textbook pregnancy. The doctor said it should be perfectly safe."

Clay paced in the small space. He walked a few steps down the hall toward the main part of the house and then spun on his heel to confront her again. "What about the family?"

"What about them?"

"They'll be worried if we're both gone."

"I've called them. I've explained everything. I said we'd be back Sunday, which we will."

"You called them."

"That's what I said."

"You told them we were both going without even discussing it with me?"

"You and I haven't done a lot of talking in the past twenty-four hours, Clay."

He ignored that. "And the reservations? The flights and the hotel room?"

"What about them?"

"You made them all for two?"

"Yes, I did."

"I don't believe this. You just assumed you were going."

"No."

"What does that mean?"

"Just what I said. I assumed nothing. I *decided* I was going."

He stared at her for a moment. Then he said in a voice as cold as dry ice, "Well, you decided wrong."

Andie kept her shoulders high, even though her back was aching and the weight of the baby seemed to drag at her. "I'm going, Clay."

"No."

"Why not?"

He leaned against the wall, rubbed his hand down his face. "Don't do this, Andie."

"What?" She bit the inside of her lip. She absolutely was not going to cry. "Don't do what? Don't stick with you when you need me?"

He looked at her some more. His eyes were old. "I do *not* need you."

That hurt. Like a knife to the heart. She winced but refused to wrap her arms around herself and cry out as she longed to do. Gently she said, "Yes, you do. You need me very badly right now. And it's my job as your wife to make sure I'm there when you *admit* you need me."

"This is ridiculous. I'll just leave without you."

"I have my own car. I'll follow you."

Clay looked away down the hall and made a scoffing sound. "I don't believe you're doing this. I thought you'd grown up. I thought you were past these selfish, grandstanding displays."

"This is not a display, Clay."

"Isn't it? I'm sorry, but from here, it looks damn dramatic, a real Andie McCreary show. Eight months pregnant and you're so noble. You'll fly to Los Angeles to be with your husband, because he *needs* you."

"It's not dramatic. It's not noble. It's just how it is. I'm going."

"No."

"Yes."

He looked so angry for a moment that she thought he was going to march over to her, grab her and shake her until she agreed to do things his way. But he didn't. His broad shoulders slumped. "Look. I just want to get through this. I just want it over with. Can't you understand?"

"Yes. I can. I do."

"Then stay here. Please."

The little section of counter that she used for folding clothes was at her back. She pressed herself against it, not resting really, but bolstering herself. She dared to ask, "Why, Clay? Why don't you want me to go?"

He closed his eyes, shook his head. "Oh, come on."

"No. Say it. Tell me."

"It's inappropriate."

"Why?"

"You know why."

"No, I don't."

"For Madeline's sake. It's cruel."

"Oh. I see. It's cruel."

"Don't be snide, Andie. It is. It's cruel."

"I don't see how. Madeline doesn't know the truth about the baby. Does she?"

"No, she doesn't."

"And you never plan for her to know, do you?"

"No."

"Then what she's never going to know won't hurt her. As far as she knows, I'm just your wife from Meadow Valley who's going to have a baby soon. *Your* baby."

There was a silence. Andie watched her husband's face. He looked so tired. The lines around his eyes seemed to have been etched deeper overnight.

He pointed out, "She's a bright woman, you know. She's going to see that you must have been pregnant before we got married."

"So? I got pregnant. And you did the right thing. Happens all the time. That's what the family thinks. Why shouldn't Madeline think the same thing?"

Clay rubbed his eyes so hard that Andie worried he would hurt them. "I don't like it." His voice was bleak. He was still slumped against the wall. He looked so awful, so drained.

Andie's determination slipped a little. Maybe she *was* in the wrong here. Maybe just giving him what he said he wanted—letting him get through this alone—would be the best thing, after all. Perhaps she'd been too hasty in deciding to go with him. She'd do better to give up and agree to stay home.

But her heart rebelled at the thought. This was the first real crisis of their married life. And Clay was a solitary type of man. The coming baby and their newlywed happiness had brought him close to her for a time. But if she let him weather this storm alone, she knew that a precedent would be set. He would never learn that he could turn to her in the difficult times.

No, she had to be there. If, while he was in Southern California, the moment came when Clay was willing to reach out for her, she couldn't afford to be five hundred miles away.

"I'm going, Clay."

"It's a mistake."

"No, it's not."

"There's no reasoning with you, is there, once you've made up your mind?"

"Not about this there isn't."

"You just do what you want to do, no matter who it hurts."

More knives, she thought. Words like knives. "I'm sorry you feel that way."

Clay let out a long, infinitely weary breath of air. "All right, Andie. We'll be late for our flight. Let's go."

Chapter Twelve

Clay hardly spoke to her during their flight. Andie tried to console herself with the thought that she'd done the right thing. If he really did need her during this awful time, she would be there.

She found the airline seats very uncomfortable. Her back seemed to be aching pretty badly, a low, deep kind of ache that was almost like cramps. She almost told Clay about it, but decided not to. He was so distant and closed off that he was sure to see any physical complaints as more "grandstanding" on her part.

When the steward came by, Andie asked him for a pillow, which she braced behind her back. It seemed to help. By the time they touched down at L.A., she felt better.

Luckily for her poor overburdened body, they had carried their luggage to their seats with them so they didn't have to wait at the baggage carousels. And then the rental car she'd ordered was ready right outside the terminal.

Clay drove them to their hotel. Andie adjusted her seat so that it pushed against the small of her back and then stretched the seat belt over her middle. She looked out the window at the palm trees and the low, red-roofed stucco houses and the towers of glass and steel in the distance.

In spite of the smog that colored the summer air gray, Andie found Los Angeles a beautiful city. It seemed to be exotic, sophisticated and sad all at once.

There were too many people wrapped in rags, pushing shopping carts piled with dirty bags. And yet the variety of humanity was fascinating to see. Barefoot men with shaved heads wearing pink robes strolled down the street beside tattooed homeboys with their billed hats on backward. And everywhere there were expensive cars, showroom perfect, driven by men who wore black-lensed sunglasses and talked very intently on their car phones as they drove.

Their hotel, the Casa de la Reina, was a Spanish-style structure with little courtyards and fountains everywhere. Bougainvillea and fragrant jasmine tumbled down the walls. Their room was on the second floor overlooking the pool.

As soon as the bellman had been tipped and was gone, Clay asked her if she was hungry.

"No. What I'd really like to do right now is put my feet up."

"That makes sense." He actually sounded noncombative, for a change. "I promised Madeline I'd call her when I got in."

Andie slipped off her shoes and sighed. "Go ahead." She climbed up on one of the two king-size beds and began arranging herself against the headboard in a sort of half-reclining posture, with pillows at her back.

"Here. Let me help." Clay grabbed more pillows off the other bed and propped up her knees, a thoughtful little gesture that she would have taken for granted just two days before.

Gratitude and love for him washed over her. She nearly drowned in it. And then the baby punched her in the stomach.

"Oh, you little scoundrel," she groaned, and touched the place where she'd been kicked.

Clay put his hand over hers. "You stop kicking your mom," he said to her stomach.

He was so close that his warmth and that subtle scent that was only him swam around her. She slipped her fingers from beneath his and reached out to cup the back of his neck, a fond gesture and an intimate one. She felt the slight toughness of the skin there, where the sun tanned him, and the blunt hairs at his nape, where his barber tapered them short. She touched the very place where his skull began.

It felt wonderful, just to have her hand on him, just to know, for that moment, that he was right there.

He looked at her. They shared a smile.

And then his glance slid away. "I should call Madeline."

"Of course."

Clay ducked out from under her touch and went to get his address book. Then he sat on the other bed and punched out the number.

Tuning out Clay's side of the conversation, Andie closed her eyes and let her mind float. But then Clay spoke to her.

"Andie?"

"Hmm?" She rolled her head and looked at him. He had his hand over the receiver.

"Madeline wants to get out. To talk. She's at her parents' house. I was thinking we could take her out to dinner."

We. He was including her, a fact that moved Andie deeply. He had made it so painfully clear that he hadn't wanted her here, yet now that she *was* here, he wasn't going to try to cut her out.

Andie considered for a moment and came to a decision. Were things different, were this baby she carried Clay's baby in every single way, she *would* have come for the funeral—but she would *not* go to dinner with them tonight. To Madeline, she was a stranger. And right now, Madeline didn't need an evening with a stranger. Madeline needed a friend. Like Clay.

Andie shook her head. "I think I'll take it easy tonight and order room service. But you go."

He frowned. "Are you sure?"

"Positive."

He looked at her closely. And then he nodded. "All right, then. I'll go alone." He tried to hide his relief, but she saw it nonetheless. He turned his attention to Madeline again.

Andie closed her eyes once more, feeling marginally better. It eased her troubled heart a little to think that, in this at least, she could do things the way Clay wanted them done.

"Hey, there."

"Huh?" She opened her eyes.

Clay was bending over her. "You went to sleep."

Andie struggled to sit up a bit higher. Her back was bothering her again and she wanted to find a position that would ease it.

"No." Clay gently guided her down. "Stay there. I just wanted you to know I'm leaving."

Her mind felt fuzzy. "I want to turn to my side."

"Okay, then." He helped her to sit. And then he moved the pillows around. "Try that."

Andie slid down and lay in her favorite sleeping position, on her side.

"Better?"

"Much." She smiled. "Now what are you doing? Leaving for dinner?"

"Right."

"Okay. Give my apologies to Madeline. Say I hope to meet her in person tomorrow."

"I will. Shall I order you something before I go? I can tell them to send it up later."

"No. I can do it when I feel like eating. You go on."

He smoothed back a few stray curls, which had clung to her cheek as she slept. "I won't be late."

His touch felt good. And her back seemed to have eased. She yawned. "Take your time." She drifted off again, hardly hearing the door close behind him.

The house where Madeline's parents lived was hidden in a small park behind a locked gate.

"Yes?" asked a disembodied voice when Clay pulled up to the gate.

He saw the speaker then, built into the stone fence at the side of the driveway. "Clay Barrett. I'm here to see Madeline."

"Come right in."

The gate made a clicking sound and swung open. He drove through.

When he saw the house, Clay thought it looked a lot like the Casa de la Reina, where he and Andie were staying. The place was huge and Mediterranean, more of a villa than anything else. Everywhere he looked he saw tropical foliage, wrought ironwork and Mexican tile.

A maid let him in. "Right this way."

He followed obediently, down a hall into a vast, airy room decorated with woven rugs, several groupings of Mission-style furniture and lots of potted palms. Clay thought of the Casa de la Reina again. The room really was like the lobby of a big hotel. An older man and a woman, seated in one of the sets of furniture, turned to look when he entered.

The woman, who had the same blond, fine-boned good looks that Madeline possessed, smiled graciously. "You must be Clay Barrett. I'm Madeline's mother, Cybil Shaeffer. And this is my husband, Madeline's father, Jim."

Jim, who looked like an aging movie star right down to the blue blazer and the ascot tie, stood and extended his arm. "Hello, Clay." He was holding a drink in his free hand. The ice cubes in it rattled. "We've heard a lot about you. It's good to meet you, even under these circumstances."

Clay shook the proffered hand. "Yes. Good to meet you, too, Mr. Shaeffer."

"Jim will do."

"Jim, then."

Jim gestured at a wrought-iron cart laden with crystal decanters. "How about a drink?"

Before Clay could answer, Madeline spoke. "Thanks, Dad. But we're leaving."

Clay turned to see her, in the arch to a hallway that began on the other side of the massive room. She wore toreador-length white pants and some kind of gauzy shirt. The straps of her wedge-heeled sandals crisscrossed over her bare ankles. She was pale, and her eyes were tired. The joyful glow that had radiated from her the last time Clay had seen her was gone.

She came toward him. "Hey, bud."

"Hey to you."

Dutifully, she kissed her parents.

"What time will you be home?" her mother asked.

"I don't know for sure, Mom. But don't worry. I'll be fine." She turned to Clay. "Shall we?"

"You bet."

They walked out of the giant room and down the long hall to the front door. Madeline's parents followed them, their shoes echoing on the tiles. They stood waving as Madeline and Clay got in the car.

"Take it easy, now," Cybil warned. "Be careful."

"We will," Madeline called to them. Then she rolled the window up and smiled a wan smile at Clay. "They hover a lot. Since it happened."

"That's normal."

"Yes. But I feel stifled already. And it's only been two days." She snapped her seat belt in place. "Now." Her voice was determinedly bright. "It's hot and it'll be light for hours yet. Can we go somewhere outside and maybe sit under a tree in the shade?"

"You bet."

Clay drove to a wild park he knew of, which was only a few miles to the west along Sunset Boulevard. The park was covered with expanses of dry grass and crisscrossed with hiking trails. Clay stopped by the side of the road and discovered a blanket in the trunk, stowed there courtesy of the rental company. They walked up a hillside and found a shady oak.

Clay spread the blanket and they sat. For a while, neither of them spoke. A hot, languid wind blew across the grass and from somewhere, quail cooed timidly to each other.

"Is this really happening?" Madeline asked at last in a wispy little voice.

Clay looked at her. Then he held out his hand. She took it.

"Yes, I'm afraid so," he said.

Madeline gave his hand a squeeze and then pulled free, as if she needed the contact, yet couldn't bear it for too long.

At the edge of the blanket, near where Madeline sat, a purple thistle grew. She touched it, touched the cruel little spikes around the blue flower.

"Will I keep living?" she asked.

He told her the truth. "Yes."

"Did anyone ever die on you, Clay?"

"Just my mother, my biological mother. When I was a kid."

"Were you there when it happened?"

"No. I was in a foster home at the time. There was some mix-up in communication. I didn't find out until she was in the ground."

"What did you feel like?"

"Angry. And lonely. I felt deserted."

Madeline's lips were pursed. "Yes. Exactly." She took in a breath that seemed painful to draw, then let it out slowly. "I'm so mad at him, Clay. So many times he left me. But this time. This way. This is forever. He's gone from the world. I think, in a way, I hate him for this. For this... ultimate recklessness. I just can't forgive it."

He understood that. Not being able to forgive Jeff.

He'd told Andie, "What he did, I'll never be able to forgive."

And Andie had said, "Oh, Clay, if you can't forgive him, how will you ever forgive me?"

"Is that awful to say, Clay?"

Clay forced himself to think of the woman beside him and not his wife. "What? That you can't forgive him?"

"Yes."

"No. It's not awful. It's just...how you feel right now."

Madeline gave him a pitiful little smile. "Thanks, Clay."

"For what?"

"For everything. For being here. For telling me that what I feel is okay."

"Hey. What are friends for?" Strange, he thought, it wasn't that difficult to sit here like this with Madeline, to listen, to say the things she needed to hear. Maybe it was because Madeline wanted nothing from him beyond acceptance and a listening ear. And he wanted nothing from her.

"Clay?"

"Yeah?"

"Clay, did something happen? Did something go wrong?"

"What do you mean?"

"Between you and Jeff?"

It took her words a few seconds to register. When they did, everything changed.

The world became ominous. The drone of insects, harmless until now, suddenly buzzed heavy with threat. The heat of the afternoon, bearable just seconds ago, was now stifling.

"Why do you ask that?" His voice seemed to tread on eggshells, it was so careful.

"Because we never saw you again, after that strange day you and Jeff went out for lunch and Jeff came back alone looking like he'd had a run-in with a meat grinder. And then, you got married. And you never even told us."

Clay looked away, across the grasses. He was stalling for time. He hadn't expected these questions from her, for the truth to rear its ugly head and demand a hearing. If he didn't tell her now, he would have to lie outright.

And yet what possible good could Madeline's knowing the truth do anyone at this point? Jeff was dead. Madeline was in a world of pain. The truth would only make the pain worse.

"Clay? What is it?"

Clay made himself look at her. "It's a long story. My wife..." He sought the right words.

She prompted, "Andie, right?"

"Yes. Andie. I mentioned on the phone today that she was pregnant, remember?"

"Yes. You said she was a little tired and wanted to rest. So she wouldn't be coming with us tonight."

"Right."

"I assumed she was being thoughtful," Madeline said. "You know, letting me have you alone, so I could cry on your shoulder."

Clay thought about that, about Andie's motives. Who could tell about Andie's motives sometimes? She'd insisted on following him here when he'd practically begged her to stay home. And yet then she'd surprised him, by backing right out of the picture when it came to this visit with Madeline. He still didn't understand what she was up to in this situation and he continued to resent the fact that she'd come.

Deep inside, maybe he was a little afraid she'd come here to say her own private goodbyes to Jeff. It made a hollow, sick place inside him, to think that she might still carry on some senseless fantasy about Jeff.

Though who could tell what went through Andie's mind? Clay certainly couldn't. Just two nights ago, she'd said she was in love with *him*. And though he didn't believe in such foolishness, it had still been satisfying to hear. He'd thought how good they had it, and even told her as much. And then Madeline called the next day.

And the world had fallen apart.

"Clay?"

He blinked. "I'm sorry."

Madeline's gray eyes were full of understanding. "Don't apologize. It's a tough time for you, too."

"Yeah, it is."

"You were saying about your wife, Andie, and about her pregnancy?"

"Right. Well, see, she was pregnant when we got married."

Madeline gave a tremulous little smile. "Oh. I get it." She actually chuckled. "Clay Barrett, you devil. You led your cousin astray."

"Er, right."

"So you're saying it all happened sort of quickly, the wedding, I mean?"

"Right. She didn't want to marry me at first."

"Ah. A woman with a mind of her own."

"Is she ever. And then, when we finally worked things out, we just wanted to have it taken care of. We went to Tahoe and did it the quick way, over a weekend."

"I see." Madeline looked knowing, but then she frowned. "But there were all those months. You never called."

"I know. It was inexcusable."

"It's not like you."

"My life, it just changed completely." In his mind, he saw Andie, laughing, holding her big stomach, rolling on the bed the other night, after she told him she loved him. Yearning welled in him, a slow, deep ache. How had it happened that she'd become so important, that she'd filled up his life? "I hope you can understand. Lately, it's just seemed like there's me and Andie and the baby. And nothing else matters. That's selfish, I know."

"Yes." Madeline's voice was soft. "Selfish. And completely understandable." She patted his hand. "It's okay. And I'm looking forward to meeting this special woman of yours tomorrow."

"I'm glad." And he was.

He was also massively relieved. Looking into Madeline's eyes, he saw that his half-truths had been believed. She wouldn't have to know about Jeff's worst betrayal, after all.

Madeline wore a dreamy, faraway look now. "You know, what I really want to do is reminisce."

"About Jeff?"

"Yes. Is that shameless and self-indulgent?"

"Absolutely. Do it."

She closed her eyes. "I will. Do you remember the time when . . . ?"

Madeline launched into a long story from the past, during their college days, when Clay and Jeff had first been friends. Clay let her tell the whole story, only stopping her when she left something out. And then he told a few old stories of his own.

Eventually, they got up and shook out the blanket and went back to the car. Madeline gave him directions to a little restaurant she knew of out at the beach. They ate dinner and watched the surf. Madeline cried and had to ask the waiter for tissues. It was near nine o'clock when they got in the rental car again.

After Clay drove through the gates and pulled up in front of her parents' house, Madeline asked him to come in.

"No, I think I'll go on back to the hotel."

Madeline leaned across the console and kissed him on the cheek. "Say hello to Andie."

"I will."

"There'll be food and, you know, people getting together, here tomorrow. After the interment."

"We'll come. Our return flight isn't until Sunday, anyway."

"Good." She leaned back against the seat. "Thanks, Clay. This helped."

"Any time."

She straightened and opened the door. He watched her run up the tile steps. Before she went inside, she turned and waved. He waved back. And then she was gone.

* * *

Twenty minutes later, Clay sat in a chair in the room at the Casa de la Reina, watching Andie sleep. The empty bed stretched between them. But his eyes had adjusted to the night. He could see her just fine. Her hair was a tousled cloud all around the side of her face and her skin looked like cream, except for the dark smudges beneath her eyes.

She'd probably tired herself out, he realized, with all the tension over the past couple of days. She was eight months' pregnant and looked like nine to him, her belly big and round, so heavy under the sheet. He sometimes thought, lately, that it must hurt her skin, to stretch that much. She rubbed creams there, he knew, to try to keep the marks to a minimum. Still, she would have a few when this was over, after the baby was out in the world.

Her arm, still slim and shapely, lay above the sheet. She wore the gold bracelet of linked hearts that she wore all the time since he'd returned from living in L.A. That bracelet seemed a part of her, a part of all that was Andie. And now that he thought of it, he didn't even know where she'd gotten it.

An old boyfriend, maybe.

It was petty of him, but he didn't like that. Didn't like to think of Andie and anyone else. Not even some long-ago high school crush.

And not Jeff. Jeff, least of all.

Jeff, who hadn't mattered, who'd been a ghost to both of them two days ago. Jeff who now, with his death, seemed to hover nearby every moment of the day and night.

Clay couldn't get his mind clear—that was the problem. He thought of Madeline, and there was hurt and sympathy. Jeff, and there was pure pain. And Andie, and there was agony.

It was all roiling around inside him. He didn't know how to get it to straighten itself out.

"Clay?" Andie's voice was sleepy, full of dreams.

He wanted to cherish her, keep her close, keep her safe. And to be inside her. He always wanted that, even now, when she was so big, when they probably shouldn't, when it might hurt the baby.

Although the doctor said it was okay and so did the books, as long as everything was all right with her.

"What are you doing, sitting there in the dark?"

"Watching you." When he made love with her, he knew he was the only one. There were no ghosts between them then. No doubts. Nothing but the two of them and a universe of pleasure.

"Is everything all right?"

"It's fine." He was hard. Aching. Wanting. And yet angry, too. He feared her, feared her power to empty out his life to nothing, if she should ever choose to leave him. And he still didn't understand why she was here, in L.A., for the funeral of the man who had used and discarded her and the baby. Not that he wanted to understand. He didn't. He was too afraid that understanding would end up hurting worse than not knowing at all.

With a little groan at the effort, she levered up on an elbow and turned on the lamp between the beds. "How did it go?"

"Fine. Where did you get that bracelet?"

"This?" She held up her right arm.

"Yeah."

A musing smile lifted the corners of her mouth. "Ruth Ann."

"What?"

She chuckled. "Well, half Ruth Ann. I saw it in the window at that jeweler's at Main and Mill streets. Ruth Ann was with me. I had half the money for it. She paid the other half. For my eighteenth-birthday present."

He grunted. "Ruth Ann." No long-lost boyfriend, after all. He wondered what was wrong with him, since Jeff had died. Always suspecting the worst. It wasn't good. "Did you eat?"

"Yep. Hours ago."

"Are you all right?"

"Yes. I'm fine. Why?"

He stood, the wanting intensifying, his hardness straining the placket of his trousers. He watched her eyes change, watched the softness and the knowing come over her.

"Oh, Clay."

"Is it a bad idea?"

He could see by her expression that she knew exactly what he meant: to make love. "No. It's just..."

"What?"

"Clay, we need to talk."

He was halfway around the end of the empty bed. He stopped there. "About what?"

She lifted her hands, a helpless gesture. "About everything. About how badly you're hurting. And how you're pushing me away."

Talking about all that was the last thing he wanted to do. He felt his desire fade to nothing, just at the thought. "It will be fine, Andie. Just let it be."

"But Clay..."

"I just need time, that's all. It will pass. In time."

"I don't know, Clay. I don't think it will. I think we have to get it out, all of it. We have to talk about Jeff, *really* talk about him. You have to let yourself admit that you didn't actually manage to cut him out of your heart and your life the way you thought you had. You have to forgive him. And then you have to forgive me."

He said nothing for a moment. His anger was a cold thing now. Then he muttered, "That's a hell of a lot that *I* have to do."

A tear spilled over her lower lid and slid down her cheek. "Clay. Please, Clay..."

"Don't." He pointed a rigid finger at her. "Just don't. I can't take it now, Andie." He started walking again, but this time he kept on going, right past her bed, into the bathroom.

"Where are you going?"

"I'm tired, Andie."

"You're running away."

He closed the bathroom door on her voice and twisted the privacy lock. He half expected her to follow him, to pound on the door, make an Andie McCreary type of scene. But all was quiet in the other room.

He took a quick shower and brushed his teeth. When he went out to the main room again, she'd turned off the light and lay on her side, facing the wall.

He didn't disturb her. Instead, he climbed into the empty bed, turned on his side away from her and closed his eyes.

As it had been the night before, his sleep was troubled. He heard Andie every time she shifted her weight in the other bed. He wanted to be there with her, beside her, to feel her leg brush his now and then and her body's warmth radiating toward him beneath the sheet whenever either of them moved.

But it was a thousand miles to that other bed. He certainly couldn't make it there in the space of a single night.

Three times, she got up and went to the bathroom. He wanted to ask if everything was okay. But he didn't. He stayed quiet. He wondered if morning would ever come. Eventually, he drifted into a shallow sleep.

Andie was already in the shower when Clay awoke. He opened his eyes and dreaded the moment when she would emerge from the bathroom.

The moment came. She appeared in a cloud of warm steamy air, wrapped in her robe that now barely covered her stomach, drying her hair with a towel.

She looked so terribly vulnerable, her body ungainly, her hair hanging in wet ropes, her skin soft from her shower. He thought again about how he wanted to protect her, to keep her and the baby safe from any harm.

And how he hadn't been doing a very good job of that the past few days.

He made himself speak. "Andie, I..."

"Please." She held up her towel for silence and she granted him a rueful smile. "Don't worry. I promise I absolutely will not bug you until we've made it through the church and the cemetery and all that stuff. I know that you've got enough to deal with right now."

His throat closed off for a moment, in gratitude and tenderness. Gruffly, he answered, "Thanks."

She lifted her shoulders in a resigned little shrug. "'S all right. What's for breakfast?"

"Room service?"

"Sounds fine."

"What do you want?"

She thought for a moment, tipping her head sideways and rubbing the ends of her hair with the towel. "Two poached and an English muffin. Tea and tomato juice. In about an hour. I want to do my hair and put on my tent." She indicated the maternity dress that was hanging in the closet area. It was navy blue, with a wide sailor collar.

Clay called the number on the room menu and ordered the food. Then he went to the bathroom to clean up himself.

Andie dried her hair and put on her makeup while Clay shaved. Then they dressed in their funeral finery. The breakfast came right on time.

After they ate, they drove together to the church. Clay wanted to be there early, to find out where he was supposed to sit or stand, what he was to do as pallbearer.

The church was a huge gothic-looking structure made of gray stone. When they'd parked the car, they went in through the massive front door. The church was quiet, hollow sounding inside. Andie sat in one of the pews while Clay went to find someone to tell him what to do.

After a while, when the baby started shifting around, Andie grew uncomfortable. So she stood and walked around a little, exploring the small sanctuaries in nooks along the side walls and studying the stained-glass windows. Up in front, the closed coffin, pristine white, was already in place. There were flowers everywhere.

Clay came and found her eventually, to explain that he would be expected to ride in one of the limousines of the cortege to the cemetery. They could make a place for her, too. But Andie told him she would prefer to take the car and follow along.

"Are you sure?"

"Yes. Don't worry. I'll be fine."

By then, it was about ten. Clay said he had a few minutes, so they sat down together. Andie looked at the coffin and all the flowers and tried to do what people did in churches, feel peaceful and serene, lifted above the everyday trials of the world. She didn't really succeed. There was too much on her mind.

Also, that uncomfortable, cramping feeling was back again. It seemed to be very low down, very deep inside. More and more she was feeling as if it wasn't her back at all. She was even starting to wonder if it could be contractions. Perhaps those contractions Clay had read to her about, the ones that took place in the last month before delivery. Braxton Hicks contractions, Andie thought they were called.

But whatever they were, they weren't that difficult to handle. She just had to relax, not let things get to her. And Monday morning, bright and early, she would give her obstetrician a call.

"Andie?" Clay's voice was very low, yet still it echoed a little in the big empty church.

"Um?"

He took her hand, squeezed it, but said nothing more. She looked at him, wondering what he hadn't said. A few days ago, she would have asked him what was on his mind. But not today. Not after last night and the way he had locked himself in the bathroom to get away from the truth.

Things were so tenuous between them. And this wasn't the time or the place to speak of their problems, anyway.

Andie closed her eyes, tipped her head up, let the rainbow of light that came through the stained-glass window above the altar bathe her face. They sat that way for a while, holding hands, saying nothing and Andie felt a little better.

Then Clay whispered to her that he'd meet her at the cemetery after the burial. From there they would drive to Madeline's parents' house for the reception.

Andie whispered back, "Okay." Clay rose and disappeared down the aisle.

Slowly, the pews filled up around her. Andie got up once before the service started to look for a bathroom. She managed to relieve herself and find another seat just in time.

The service was short. The minister read from the psalms and talked about Jeff. Around her, Andie heard people sniffling and those tight little sounds that happen when someone is trying not to cry out loud.

When it was over, Clay and five other young men surrounded the coffin. They lifted it between them and carried it down the aisle. The ushers led the family members out and then the rest of the mourners followed.

To Andie, the ride to the cemetery took forever, much longer than the service had taken. Driving was becoming more difficult all the time now, with her huge stomach nearly pressing against the steering wheel. And the line of cars was long and slow.

But at last, she arrived at the place where Jeff would be buried. She found a parking space with reasonable ease and joined the others, who had regrouped around the grave site. There were some folding chairs set up, in two groups beneath a pair of canopies. By then, all the chairs were taken.

Being as big as a house had advantages, though. An older gentlemen who spoke with a charming Irish brogue gave Andie his seat. She thanked him and sank gratefully into it.

Andie watched Clay, who was standing right by the grave where the coffin was already set. He was looking around, his expression tense and concerned. She didn't realize he was looking for her until their eyes met. His face smoothed out. She gave him a smile and a tiny wave.

The minister spoke again, reciting more verses from the Bible. And then a slim blond woman stepped forward. Madeline. She put a single rose on top of the huge bouquet that was already covering the coffin. They lowered the coffin into the ground. Madeline threw a handful of dirt on it. The minister said words of benediction.

Slowly, the mourners began to move away, singly and in groups. Andie sat in her chair, waiting for Clay. Finally he came. She led him to the car and they drove to the reception.

"Are you all right?" Clay asked her when they'd driven through a wrought-iron gate and parked in the driveway that was lined with cars.

Andie looked at him, thinking, *That's all we do lately— ask each other if we're all right.*

Down inside that tightness came. Like a hand in there, turning to a fist. Not that hard to bear, but definitely worrisome. She breathed deeply. The tightness eased.

"Andie?"

She gave him the answer he wanted to hear. "I'm fine. Let's go in."

The big house was full of flowers and people. Andie left Clay soon after they were shown in the door. She found a bathroom and felt better after she'd used the toilet and rinsed her face.

Then she waddled her way down several hallways to the big living room, where most of the people were. The nice older man who'd given her his chair at the cemetery introduced himself. His name was Bob and he was a great-uncle of Madeline's, on her father's side. He asked Andie if she'd like something to drink.

Andie smiled gratefully and requested some mineral water. The man disappeared down a hallway. Andie found a vacant chair of dark rich wood with studded leather cushions. It seemed suitable to be the throne of a Spanish grandee. She lowered her bulk into it.

As she waited for her mineral water, Andie watched the people. Most of them seemed older and, judging by their jewelry and clothing, quite well-to-do. There were a few children, dressed in somber colors but irrepressible nonetheless, as children usually are. They played tag in the long hall that Andie could see to her left, and giggled and chased each other around the heavy, dark furniture. Every once in a while, an adult would grab a little arm and tell the pint-size culprit to settle down. For a few moments, there would be sedate good behavior. And then the fun would start again.

"Hello."

Andie turned from watching a little girl playing peeka-boo behind an areca palm to see the woman she knew to be Madeline standing by her chair.

"You're Andie, aren't you?"

Andie started to stand. "Yes, I—"

"No. Don't get up." Madeline was looking at Andie's stomach. "Please."

Andie chuckled. "Great idea." She sank back into the chair. "Madeline?"

"Yes."

Andie stuck out a hand. "Glad to meet you."

"Me, too."

Their hands clasped briefly, then both let go. At the same time, they both began, "I've heard so much about—" And then they laughed, in unison.

Madeline said, "Thanks for lending me your husband's shoulder last night."

"I hope it helped."

"It did."

They looked at each other, strangers yet connected. They didn't know what to say to each other, but both felt the link. Andie decided she liked Madeline's eyes. There was great kindness in them. Goodness seemed to radiate from her.

Andie thought of Jeff. A fool, to have chanced losing this woman, she thought. The ultimate fool to have thrown it all away in the end for a fast ride in a new car.

Graceful and slim, Madeline pulled up a nearby hassock and perched on it. Andie watched the lithe movement longingly. Would she ever be thin again?

Madeline leaned close. "I have to tell you. When Clay said you two had gotten married, I wasn't surprised."

"You weren't?"

"No. Sometimes he used to talk about you, his willful and troublemaking cousin Andie. I thought then that his feelings about you were more than cousinly. But I also knew if I pointed it out, he'd glare at me and tell me to mind my own business, that I was way off."

"So you didn't point it out?"

"Right. I'm no fool."

Bob reappeared carrying the promised mineral water. Andie thanked him and took the glass.

"Anything," Bob declared, "for a sweet Irish colleen."

"Uncle Bob," Madeline groaned. "Honestly. He thinks everybody's an Irish colleen."

Andie took a sip of her water. "Well, he's half-right. My mom's Italian, but my dad's Irish."

"Sure, and what did I tell you?" Uncle Bob laid it on thick.

"I'll just bet," Madeline said.

"It's true," Andie assured her. "McCreary. That was my last name, before I married Clay. About as Irish as they come."

Uncle Bob remarked that he believed McCreary was a Scots name. Before Andie could argue with him, Clay appeared.

"*There* you are," Clay said from behind her chair. "I was looking all over."

Andie tipped her head back and smiled up at him. "I was just listening to a little blarney from Uncle Bob here, and Madeline and I—"

Andie cast a swift, conspiratorial glance toward Madeline. What she saw made her look again.

Madeline was on her feet. "McCreary?" she said softly. "Andie for *Andrea?*" Her face was dead white.

"Yes," Andie said. "Andie for Andrea."

"I see," Madeline said. "And just when is your baby due?"

Andie blinked. Madeline looked so strange. "I, um..."

Madeline waved a limp hand in the air. "Never mind. Now I think about it, I don't believe I really want to know." Then her eyes rolled back and her knees buckled.

Somehow Uncle Bob managed to catch her before she hit the tiled floor.

Chapter Thirteen

At once, the whole sprawling room was a beehive of frantic activity.

"Oh, my sweet Lord!" a woman cried.

"What is it? What's happened?"

"It's Madeline. She's fainted."

"What?"

"Step back everyone, give her air."

"Bob, follow me. To her room. This way."

Andie watched, clutching the arms of her chair, as Madeline was carried away.

"What in the world happened?" A painfully slim woman with rather wild-looking, curly gray hair asked Andie.

Clay was the one who answered. "We don't know."

"But what did she say? What were you talking about?" The woman tipped her head to the side, a birdlike movement, curious and alert.

"Nothing, just small talk," Clay insisted.

The woman, however, wasn't taking Clay's word for it. Her little brown eyes were on Andie. Andie struggled to give her some kind of response. "Clay's right. We don't know what happened. She, um, asked me when the baby was due and then..."

The woman finally saw that Andie was almost as distressed as poor Madeline. "There, there, dear." Her voice had become soothing. "Don't *you* go getting all upset. I'm sure she'll be fine. It's just the stress, you know. She loved Jeffrey so."

"I'm sure it must be awful for her," Andie heard herself murmur.

"But she'll survive. Madeline is very strong. Very strong, indeed."

"Yes, I'm sure she is," Andie agreed.

There was a moment of awkward silence, then the woman launched into the amenities. "Oh, I'm sorry. I didn't even tell you who I am. My name is Suzanne. Suzanne Corey. Jeffrey's mother was my cousin." She held out a thin, veiny hand.

Andie took the hand and murmured her own name. "And this is my husband, Clay."

Suzanne nodded at Clay. "You were Jeffrey's friend, right?"

"Yes."

"It's so hard to believe," she said in sad little whisper.

"Yes," Andie agreed.

"He was so young, so vital. And now he's gone. All the Kirklands, gone now."

"Yes," Andie said again, not knowing quite what else to say.

"But Jeffrey was always a little wild. Too much of a risk taker." Suzanne glanced at Clay. "Do you know what I mean?" She went on before Clay could say anything. "He had it all. He was bright and handsome and there was always plenty of money. And everyone loved him. How could we not? He was so very full of life, brimming with it. Always. I'm sure you remember."

"Yes." Clay's voice sounded a little hoarse, Andie thought. "I remember."

"And then there was Madeline. A wonderful girl. They grew up together, did you know?"

"Yes. I know."

"But somehow it wasn't enough. It was just never enough. And it was hard on him, to lose both of his parents so close together, even if he was a grown man. He felt very alone then, I think." Suzanne shook her head. "Poor dear boy."

Right then, a tall man put his arm around Suzanne's narrow waist and bent to whisper something in her ear.

Suzanne nodded, "Yes, I know. All right." She looked at Clay and Andie. "This is my husband, Lou."

Andie and Clay nodded and said hello.

Suzanne smiled fondly at her husband. "Lou says I talk too much." Lou looked down on her indulgently. "And maybe he's right. Well." She was suddenly brisk. "We have to be on our way now. I do hope we meet again."

"Yes, nice to meet you," Lou said. Then he took Suzanne's arm and off they went.

As soon as Suzanne and Lou were out of earshot, Clay bent near Andie's ear and asked, "Are you ready to go?"

Andie was more than ready. But it didn't seem right, somehow. "No. We should stay. We should see that she's okay."

"Do you really think it's necessary?"

"Yes."

He let out a long breath. "All right." In spite of his eagerness to get out of there, she knew he agreed with her. They should stay.

And they did, though each minute seemed like a year. Finally, half an hour later, Madeline returned.

The moment she entered the room, everybody, even the children, grew quiet. Then slowly the conversations began again. Madeline went from guest to guest, touching and hugging, reassuring everyone that she was just fine.

"She's all right," Clay said in Andie's ear.

"Yes."

"I think we should go." There was dread in his voice. He knew, of course, that something had happened, that Madeline had come to some awful realization. And he didn't want to learn what.

Probably because, in his heart, he already knew.

"No." Andie reached up and patted his hand, which rested on the back of her chair. "Wait. She'll work her way around to us."

And slowly she did.

"I'm sorry." Madeline's smile was distant and gracious. "It's a hard time. I hope you understand."

Andie looked in the other woman's eyes, saw denial, saw the desperate plea that she say nothing at all of what they both knew had really happened.

"We do. We understand completely," Clay said.

"Yes." Andie smiled, a smile as distant as Madeline's. She saw a little of the tension leave Madeline's face. "And we really have to be going."

Madeline simulated regret. "Oh, no. Not so soon."

"Yes." Andie levered her heavy body to a standing position. Then she took Madeline's hand. Madeline allowed that, though Andie felt her flinch. "Take care of yourself. Please," Andie said.

"Oh, I will." Madeline's smile looked as if it could break right off her face and fall, shattering into a thousand sharp pieces, to the tiles below.

Clay came around the chair. Dutifully, Madeline lifted her cheek to be kissed. Clay brushed his lips against her skin.

"Keep in touch now," Madeline chided. Both Andie and Clay knew what those words were worth: nothing. Madeline was only making the noises people make when they don't dare say what's really on their minds.

"She knows." Andie waited to say the truth until after they had returned to their hotel room.

Clay tossed his jacket on a chair and yanked his tie off as it were strangling him. "You can't be sure of that."

"I can. I am. And so are you."

"Look. What's the point in talking about this? We don't know *what* she knows. We'll probably never know."

Andie gaped at her husband for a moment, wanting to strangle him. Then she kicked her shoes into the corner of the open closet area and lumbered into the bathroom, closing the door behind her

When she came out wearing her robe, Clay had changed into jeans, a T-shirt and running shoes. He was sprawled in one of the chairs next to the small table by the window, drinking a beer from the beverages that were stored in the half refrigerator beneath the sink of the room's small courtesy bar.

Andie hung up her dress and decided she could use a drink, too. So she got herself a ginger ale. Then she went to the bed she'd been using and began moving her pillows around.

"You want some help with that?"

Andie turned to look at Clay. "No. I can manage." She crawled up on the bed and settled in, then treated herself to a little ginger ale. After one long refreshing drink, she set the bottle on the stand between the beds and looked at her husband defiantly. "Madeline knows about the baby, Clay. I saw it in her eyes."

Clay drank from the beer, draining it. Then he admitted, "Maybe. But what can we do about it if she does? There's just no point in stewing about it. Let it be."

"I am not stewing. I just want you to admit that—"

He sighed. "How? How could she know? Nothing at all was said. Except that your maiden name is McCreary and Andie stands for Andrea. How do you figure she *knows* from that?"

"I saw her face. I know she knows. And so do you."

Clay got up, lean, unfettered, his body hard and proud. As she had envied Madeline, Andie envied him. She felt so huge and slow just watching him move. One of those strange, contractionlike cramps gripped her. She grabbed one of her pillows, clutched it against herself, to her heart.

Clay didn't even notice what was happening to her. He was striding to the refrigerator, bending to yank the door open. When he had another bottle in his hand, he straightened with his back to her, shoved the refrigerator door closed with his leg and knocked off the bottle cap with the opener that was built into the side of the counter. By then, the cramp, or whatever it was, had crested and was fading away. Still not facing her, Clay tipped the bottle and drank from it.

Andie stared at his back, wondering if she should tell him what had just happened. But no, it really hadn't been that bad. Like the other contractions, it was one she had ridden out easily. It was nothing to be too concerned about, she was sure. But if she mentioned it to Clay, he'd make a big deal about it. And he'd use it to end this painful—but important—conversation.

Gently Andie reiterated, "Madeline knows the truth, Clay."

That did it. He turned around and faced her. His eyes were like cold green stones. "All right, fine. Madeline knows. Isn't that terrific?"

Andie chose to ignore the sarcasm. "It will take her some time, but I'm sure we'll be hearing from her."

Clay made a disgusted sound. "What the hell are you talking about? We'll never see or hear from Madeline again."

"You're wrong."

He stared at her for a long time. Then he swore and drank some more.

Andie wanted to cry. But she didn't. She dared to try once more. "We have to talk, Clay. We can't go on pretending that nothing's wrong between us."

His hand shot up, palm out. "Stop. Right there."

"But we—"

"No." He turned enough to set his beer down, hard, on the counter, then he glared at her once more. "Listen. You just listen. For a change."

Andie bit her lip. "All right."

"You just had to get me to admit that Madeline knows about the baby. All right. I've admitted it. But why stop there? You're so brave and honest, let's take it all the way. Let's examine *why* she knows."

Andie suddenly found she couldn't look at him. She was still holding the pillow. She clutched it tighter. "I—"

He cut her off before she even started. "Right. Look away."

"I'm not, I—"

"Fine. Then face it. She knows because of *you*, Andie. Because you just *had* to come here. Because you wouldn't do as I asked you to do and stay home where you belong right now."

That hurt. Badly. The pillow Andie hugged brought no comfort against that. Again in her mind, she saw Madeline, pale faced, slowly sinking to the floor. And Madeline later, with her brittle, ghastly smile, reminding them to keep in touch.

Oh, yes. Clay was right. Andie had begged for honesty. And he was giving it to her. It had been a bad call for her to come here. Those awful moments at the reception never had to happen.

Clay wasn't through. He demanded, "What's going on, Andie? What the hell are you up to?"

She made herself meet his eyes, *willed* him to believe. "I just wanted to be with you. I swear. I wanted to be here for you, in case you needed me."

He grunted. She could see he wasn't buying. How in the world could she convince him that her motives had been true ones when he simply refused to believe her every time she tried to explain? "I want to get something clear right now." Clay leaned back against the counter, his hands behind him, gripping the counter rim. "I want to be sure you hear it. Are you listening?"

"Yes."

"Okay. Look. I *am* angry at you. For coming here. But I want you to know that I can live with that. I'll get over that. If you'll just... get off me for a while. Just let it go. You did what you did and that's that. We have to go on from here. There's no sense in belaboring all of this. As I keep trying to make you see, there is nothing more to talk about."

"But there is. There's—"

"I'm not finished."

"I... okay."

"I don't know what happens with you sometimes. I don't understand why you do what you do. And it doesn't matter."

"Yes, it does. It does matter." She put everything she had into those words.

He only shook his head and looked down at his shoes, waiting for her outburst to end. When she said nothing more he looked up. "Are you through?"

Bleakly, she nodded.

"Okay, then. I don't like that you came here, but you *did* come here. It's done. And as for the rest, well, it's *my* problem and I have to handle it." He rubbed at his eyes, scrubbed his hair back from his forehead. "Jeff is dead. And for some reason, I'm having a little trouble dealing with it. But I *will* deal with it."

"But Clay—"

"No. Hear me out." He waited. She said nothing. He went on. "I want you to know that I believe in your basic integrity, Andie. I swear I do. I know that you've been a good wife to me, that you'll continue being a good wife. We'll get on with our lives. And everything will work out well enough in the end."

He appeared to have finished. For a moment, there was quiet.

She asked, her tone carefully controlled, "May I speak now?"

He shrugged.

"Thank you. I think you're wrong. Very wrong. I don't believe that everything is just going to work out by itself. I think we have to tell the truth. All the truth. To each other. I think we have to drag it out into the light and look at it and see what it really is."

"What truth? I know the truth. There's nothing more to say about it."

"Yes, there is. And you know there is. I want us to talk, Clay. Really talk. You say that I do things you don't understand. And I say I'm willing to explain those things to you. But you don't want to hear. That doesn't make any sense, Clay. It won't work. You have to know. I have to tell you. About Jeff and New Year's Eve. About what happened, why I—"

"No!" He seemed to realize he had shouted the word, and lowered his voice to a near whisper. "There's no need for that. No need at all."

"But there *is.*"

His jaw was set. "I've said all I'm going to say on this subject. Drop it. Just let it go."

She stared at him, thinking about walls, the walls they'd breached for a golden time. The walls that were so high and impenetrable now. Andie felt as if she were clawing at those walls, raking her nails bloody. But they were made of stone, impervious to her feeble efforts to batter them down with her two soft hands.

And she felt so tired. Tired and huge and ponderous. The baby seemed to drain her, to demand everything of her. She didn't have enough of herself left right now to keep battling Clay like this. And it couldn't be good for the baby, all this tension and frustration. She had to take care of herself, not allow herself to become so upset.

She met his eyes. "All right, Clay. Have it your way."

She saw relief on his face—and something else, too. What was it? Disappointment? Despair?

She didn't know, was just too tired to try anymore to keep fighting and find out.

"Are you hungry?" he asked.

"No. I just want a nap. A long nap."

He was suddenly all solicitude, helping her to lie down in the bed, fluffing her pillows. When she was settled, he touched her cheek. "You have to take care of yourself." He echoed her own thoughts.

"I know." She sighed, understanding with a stab of regret that his kindness, his attentiveness, were her rewards for not saying what needed to be said. She thought of all those years they'd been enemies. Had she been wiser then than now, to keep him at bay with hostility? Had something inside her always known how dangerous it would be to give her heart to a man like him, a man who refused even to believe that the very special love she bore him was real?

Gently he asked, "Are you going to be okay?"

"Yes, I'm fine."

"There's a gym in the basement. I thought maybe I'd—"

She completed his sentence for him. "Go work off a little tension?"

"Yeah. More or less."

"Sounds like a great idea. Do some sit-ups for me." She closed her eyes.

His lips brushed her forehead. "I will." He left her and moved around the room, changing into shorts, she imagined, getting ready to go. She heard the door close behind him just as another contraction took hold down inside her. But it faded quickly. Not real labor. Surely not.

Minutes later, she was asleep.

When Clay returned, they ordered room service and watched a movie. The contractions Andie had been experiencing became more frequent and pronounced as the evening went by. It became impossible to hide them from Clay. He wanted to call the doctor in Meadow Valley.

Andie soothed him. They should wait until tomorrow. If the contractions were still happening in the morning, they would get hold of the doctor somehow, and ask his advice before she got on a plane. But it was very possible that a good night's rest would make all the difference. And really, she was getting along in the pregnancy. These were probably the normal contractions that a mother often felt in her last month as her body begin readying itself to give birth.

Rather unwillingly, Clay accepted her judgment about it.

They went to bed at dusk, planning to be up before dawn since their flight was an early one.

But in the middle of the night, Andie awoke from a dream where some awful, cackling, witchlike person was pressing on her stomach. She dragged herself to a sitting position and pushed her hair away from her face.

Clay, who had lain down next to her at bedtime, sat up beside her.

"What is it?"

"Nothing, really. I just...I think I want to go to the bathroom, that's all." She slid off the far side of the bed and edged her way toward the bathroom.

And then something stunning happened. Her uterus contracted, from the top down. It was the most incredible thing she had ever experienced. She could feel it, moving like a living thing, over her extended belly and down to the depths of her.

"Oh!"

"My God. Andie, what—?"

And then something gave. Inside. She looked down. There was liquid trickling between her legs.

Clay was out of the bed and at her side in seconds. He put his arm around her shoulders, pulled her close against his solid strength. "What? Tell me. Please, Andie."

"I think..."

"What?"

"I think my water just broke."

Chapter Fourteen

"What are you telling me?" Clay demanded.

The doctor regarded him warily, probably because he'd sounded so harsh. She was an attractive red-haired woman with a stethoscope around her neck and a white jacket over her clothes. She wore a name tag: Dr. A. F. Johannson, Obstetrics and Gynecology.

Clay reminded himself that he needed this woman on his side. "I'm sorry, Dr. Johannson. I'm...not at my best right now."

The doctor's freckled face relaxed. "I understand. And what I'm telling you is that your wife is in active labor."

Clay blinked and shook his head. He'd known that *something* was happening, of course. He didn't have to be a doctor to understand that the baby was probably coming. But the mad rush through the dark streets to the nearest hospital hadn't left him a lot of room for thinking. And now, actually hearing the word *labor* made it suddenly all too real.

Clay struggled to recall what all those books had told him. "*Active* labor?" he asked rather idiotically.

"Yes," Doctor Johannson replied. And then she began speaking calmly and clearly about the high quality of care the obstetrics wing of this particular hospital would provide, about nonstress tests, about effacement and dilatation, about the baby's presentation and the frequency of Andie's contractions. Clay hardly understood a word of it. All those books he'd read to be prepared for this moment were totally useless to him now that the moment was actually here.

All he could say was, "Is she all right? Is the baby all right? It's early. She's not due for—"

"A few weeks yet—we know. But so far, we're doing just great. The baby seems to be okay and is in a fine position. And Andie's a real trooper."

"A trooper." Clay looked at Dr. Johannson as if he'd never heard that word before.

The doctor gave him an understanding smile. "What I'm saying is, so far, so good."

"Can I go be with her now? I've filled out every damn form they shoved under my nose."

"Yes. She's in our labor room at this point. You may go in there as you are. But when the time comes to move Andie to delivery, you'll have to scrub down and wear a gown."

"Fine. Whatever. Where is she?"

Clay was led down two or three hallways to a big room with several beds in it. There was a woman in one of the beds moaning and crying out in a language Clay didn't understand. Andie lay in another bed, on her side, turned away from him.

He went to her. "Andie?"

She opened her eyes and forced a smile. Her face looked so tired, swollen and oily with sweat. A contraction gripped her. She moaned and her hand clawed for his. He gave it and then somehow managed to murmur something soothing and soft as she ground his bones together with her grip.

When the contraction passed, she panted, "Clay, I'm sorry. You were right. I make such bad, thoughtless decisions. I shouldn't have come here, should I? I should have stayed home, not put myself and the poor baby under such stress."

He agreed with her. In fact, he feared he would always nurse a certain resentment against her for her reckless foolishness in all this. She was just like Jeff, doing what she wanted, no matter what the consequences. But now was not the time to think of all that.

He repeated what the doctor had told him. "They say it's going to be all right, Andie. They say the baby is fine."

"But what if—?"

"Shh." He made his voice tender. "No *what ifs*. The baby is fine and you're fine. That's what matters now. Relax."

"They hooked me up to a monitor before they brought me in here."

"And?"

"They said what you said. No signs of fetal distress."

"See?" He smoothed sweat-damp hair back from her face. "What did I tell you?"

Andie didn't get a chance to answer, because another contraction took her voice away. Her hand was in his. He didn't let go. He concentrated on what he'd learned in their childbirth classes and forgot all the reasons he was frustrated with her.

Andie needed him. And so did the baby. And for now, that was all that mattered.

* * *

They stayed in that room for four and a half hours.

For Clay, everything blended together. The whole world centered down to the woman moaning and wailing from the other bed, Andie's clutching hand and those strange, dreamlike periods that came between the contractions. Then, Andie would ask Clay to rub her back or she would take sips of water or even stagger to the commode behind the door at one end of the room.

And then, at last, Dr. Johannson returned, examined Andie and said that she could start pushing, something Andie had been begging Clay to let her do for what seemed like half a lifetime. Since this was Andie's first baby, she started pushing right there in the labor room.

When Clay could actually see a tiny bit of the baby's head between contractions, Dr. Johannson, who was sticking close by now, said it was time to for Andie to be moved.

Clay was led away to a place where he could scrub his hands. Then, wearing hospital greens, he was taken to the delivery room where Andie already was.

It was there that he truly began to understand why, for generation upon generation, labor and birth had been the province of women. It was simply too much for the average guy to take.

But somehow Clay did take it. And in the end, he was caught up in the excitement, the sense of exhilaration, as each of Andie's contractions brought the baby closer to the world. The doctor stayed beside Andie, monitoring the baby's heart rate after each contraction.

And Andie seemed changed now, totally exhausted, yet suffused with a hot, powerful kind of energy. When the baby's head had crowned and no longer sank back inside between contractions, things moved with alarming rapidity. At the last minute, tearing seemed imminent, so the episiotomy they'd hoped to avoid was performed, after all. Andie took it well, though Clay found he had to look away.

The rest was fast. The head emerged, red and angry, wet with blood and fluids. The doctor guided the shoulders out. The rest of the baby followed quickly.

It was a *she*. Clay, who had been allowed to catch the tiny body as it emerged, could hardly believe that he was holding her. Her eyes were scrunched closed. And she let out a big, angry wail.

"A girl," said the delivery nurse, who quickly scooped the child away from him. "Skinny, from lack of finishing time. But the lungs are just fine from the sound of that wail."

The afterbirth came as they clamped the cord. Clay only stared, stuck midway between awe and nausea. Then they laid the tiny, messy creature on Andie's breast while down below the doctor went to work sewing up the incision she'd made. "Emily," Clay heard Andie say in a soft voice. "We'll call her Emily." She looked for Clay, found him. "Is that okay with you?"

He nodded, since right then his throat was too tight to allow words to come.

Clay spent the next half hour on the phone, calling Andie's mother and his mother, and, of course, Ruth Ann. He assured them all that both Andie and the new baby were fine and said he didn't know how long it would be until they came home. A few days, at the very least.

His aunt Thelma was ready to hop the next flight south, but Clay convinced her to wait until at least tomorrow when they'd have a better idea of how long Andie and the baby would have to be in the hospital.

When he hung up from the final call, Clay dropped into the plastic hospital chair that was right there by the phone and stared at the wall for a few minutes.

"Hey, fella, you through?"

There was a man standing over him, waiting to use the phone.

"Yeah. Sure. Go ahead." Clay staggered to his feet.

He wandered off down the hall like a man in a trance. After walking for several minutes, he took an elevator down two floors and then, by instinct perhaps, found himself at the door to the cafeteria.

Clay went through the line and bought scrambled eggs, wheat toast and a big cup of black coffee. He sat down and ate. The toast was slightly soggy and the eggs reminded him of something he used to play with as a kid—Goofy Putty, he thought it was called. But it was eleven in the morning and he hadn't eaten since early last night. After everything that had happened, his body craved fuel.

When the food was gone, he went back to the obstetrics floor. The nurse told him where Andie was, that they'd just moved her to one of the private rooms. The nurse pointed out the room.

Clay went in and found Andie asleep. He stood over her for a few moments, thinking how drained she looked and yet peaceful, too.

Her right hand was outside the blanket, the hearts-of-gold bracelet gleaming there along with the plastic identity band the hospital had snapped on. When they'd first arrived in emergency, the admitting clerk had tried to convince Andie to give the gold bracelet to Clay for safekeeping, or at least allow the hospital to store it in their safe.

"No way," Andie had informed the clerk. "This is my lucky bracelet."

The clerk had given in.

Clay stared at the linked hearts, feeling a little bit guilty. He'd jumped to conclusions about that bracelet at first. In fact, if he hadn't asked her where it came from, he probably would have been eaten up with jealousy when she wouldn't part with it. He'd have been positive that she cherished it because an old flame had given it to her. And in reality, the "old flame" had only been Ruth Ann.

He should be more understanding of her—he could see that. And yet, she *was* reckless. She did throw herself into things, never considering the cost.

Because of her ill-considered decisions, Madeline had been compelled to endure even more suffering. And the baby had been forced into the world ahead of time.

Both Madeline and the baby would survive.

But look at Jeff. A sharp pain twisted inside him at the thought of the dead man. In the end, Jeff hadn't survived the consequences of his own recklessness.

Jeff had been dangerous to know, in the truest sense of the word. He'd left heartbreak in his wake.

And Andie was the same.

A small sigh escaped Andie's lips. She turned her head on the pillow but didn't open her eyes.

Clay watched her, as it seemed he had always watched her, his emotions all tangled and knotted inside him. Bemused. Aching. Confused. Resentful. So many feelings, so much turmoil in his life. Because of her.

Yet to consider his world without her now was to imagine emptiness. A blasted, forsaken terrain.

So he wouldn't consider that. Ever. She belonged with him, and he with her. Eventually, this anger and hurt he felt every time he looked at her would fade. Time would do that.

They didn't need to do any more talking, as she seemed to think. They didn't need to dredge up all the hurtful details of her brief love affair with his ex-best friend.

They just needed to forget it. It was over. That was all.

Clay bent and lightly kissed his wife's forehead. She mumbled something and turned to her side, tugging at the blanket with one hand. He helped her, pulling up the cover and tucking it around her chin.

She murmured something else. It sounded like "Thanks."

"You're welcome." He hardly breathed the words. And then he quietly left the room.

He went to see Emily next. They'd cleaned her up and she was in the nursery. They told him he could look through the observation window. Or, if he would scrub down again and put on another gown, they'd let him in among the rows of tiny beds to hold her.

Clay washed and dressed in green. And then they let him in with her. He stood over her and looked down at her, all swaddled up tight in a white blanket. Then the nursery aide lifted her and handed her over.

She was so light, like a warm puff of air in his arms.

A tiny red fist wearing an armband like Andie's broke free of the blankets and waved at him. Clay touched that fist, so soft and wrinkled and powdery dry with its perfect tiny nails. It instantly opened and closed around his finger in a strong, needful grip.

"Yes," he whispered. "Yes, I'm here. I'll always be here."

And Emily opened her eyes. She looked at him. Something happened in the deepest part of him. It was as if she reached down into him with that tiny perfect hand of hers and took hold of his heart.

He saw Andie in the shape of her jaw and the curve of her mouth. Perhaps he even saw Jeff around the eyes. But those were physical things, insignificant to Clay against the enormity of what he looked at.

He looked at Emily. A person in her own right. And she looked back at him.

He bent close to her so that the baby smell of her surrounded him and he whispered his vow to her. "I won't leave you. I'm right here. You will have what matters. A mother and a father to love you and pay attention to you and teach you what life should be."

She seemed to grip his finger all the tighter. He rubbed her hand against his own cheek. She made a little sound, a gurgling, cooing noise.

Clay looked up. The aide was watching him, a fatuous smile on her face.

"You'll be a good father," the woman said quietly. "I can tell just by watching you. And your daughter is a beautiful child."

Three days later, Andie and Emily were released from the hospital. Before they left, Clay signed the birth certificate as he had sworn he would do. Thelma, who had flown down the day before, was there to help with the mountain of equipment having a new baby seemed to require.

They rode straight to the airport and boarded the plane for home. The flight was uneventful, aside from the fuss the flight attendants made of the newborn.

At home, since Della and Ruth Ann had been hard at work getting things ready, all was in order. It was decided that during these first days, Emily would stay near her mother in the master bedroom. Della had bought a bassinet for this purpose. With great pomp and ceremony, mother and daughter were installed in their beds.

Seeing that the women had everything under control, Clay went to the office to relieve his father, who had stepped in temporarily while they were in L.A. Thelma, who had already decided that she would stay over in one of the spare rooms for a while, made lunch for everyone and began planning the dinner menus for the next week.

Over the days that followed, Andie was grateful for her mother's help and support. Thelma cooked and cleaned and sympathized with her daughter unstintingly when Andie's breasts were sore from nursing and when Andie looked at her pouchy stomach in the bathroom mirror and burst into tears.

"I kept waiting to be thin again," Andie wailed. "And look at me. I'm like an empty paper sack."

"It will go down," her mother assured her.

Andie was shameless. "You promise me, Mom?"

Thelma was, too. "Absolutely. I guarantee it. Especially if you start exercising soon."

"I will. I swear I will."

From the bedroom, Emily started to wail.

Andie groaned, thinking about the pain when that small mouth latched on to her breast.

"You could go ahead and switch to formula," Thelma suggested gently, reading correctly the expression on her daughter's face.

"No, just a few more days and it won't hurt anymore. All the books say so."

On the second Monday in September, when Emily was a little over two weeks old, Thelma went back to her own house. Joe wanted his wife back. Like everyone else, Andie's father adored his granddaughter. But he was tired of sleeping alone and foraging in the freezer when dinnertime came.

Andie was feeling much stronger by then. She took over the maintenance of her own house without much difficulty. She was even able to start dropping in at the office for a few hours twice a week or so, since Thelma was more than happy to keep an eye on Emily for a while.

And Clay was wonderful, he really was. He worked all day. Yet in the middle of the night, when Emily cried, he would get up and check for a full diaper, even rock her before waking Andie for the feeding that was usually required.

Looking back in later years, Andie remembered those first weeks of Emily's life as a stressful yet magical time. A time during which Emily daily performed miracles. She kicked her arms and legs; she gurgled and cooed. Clay swore she smiled, though Thelma insisted that was only gas.

Andie would have been happy. She *was* happy. Except for the distance between herself and Clay. A distance that, somehow, seemed to inch a little wider every day.

Clay ate breakfast across from her. He went to work and came home right on time—there were no more detours to Doolin's pub. He slept beside her. He was kind and considerate and always ready to do whatever she asked of him.

Except to let her beyond the wall.

Three and a half weeks after Emily's birth, the doctor gave Andie the go-ahead to resume, as he put it, "intimate relations." He even fitted her for a cervical cap, which she went right to the drugstore and bought. She felt so nervous and happy at the prospect of making love with Clay once again.

That night, Andie told her husband what the doctor had said. Clay patted her arm and muttered something about that being fine.

And that was all. The next day he left for Lake Tahoe for a week of continuing-education classes, which were necessary for him to keep his CPA license.

Andie told herself that as soon as Clay returned, they would rediscover the physical side of their marriage.

But when he came back, they rediscovered nothing. Over the next weeks, she tried dropping subtle hints, cuddling up against him, even asking him outright if there was something wrong that he didn't seem to desire her anymore. Clay managed to be vague and distant and neither answer her questions nor respond to her attempts to arouse his interest.

Sometimes Andie dared to imagine that he looked at her with the old hunger in his eyes. But it was always just a glance, quickly masked. It could have been no more than wishful thinking.

There were certainly no other signs that he had any interest in her sexually. Though Clay slept in their bed with her, he kept to his side of it. It almost seemed as if he was making a conscious effort not to let his body so much as brush against hers.

How could she get close to him when he so constantly kept her at bay?

The answer was, she couldn't.

At least, that was what Clay hoped.

Because he was doing just what she suspected. He was keeping clear of her physically. It was driving him nuts, but he was doing it.

Clay was determined to avoid making love with her for as long as he could hold out. Too much happened when he made love with her. He was weakened by the sexual power she had over him.

He knew her too well. With Andie, physical intimacy and emotional intimacy were one and the same. As soon as they made love, she'd be at him, wanting to talk about things he never even wanted to think of again, wanting to root around in the past like a pair of emotional archaeologists at some major dig.

Clay didn't want to do it. He wasn't *going* to do it.

But, damn, he did want her.

If he believed in such things, he would have sworn she was a witch, that she'd put some sort of sex spell on him so he'd finally go crazy from wanting her so much.

And he knew she was exercising to get back in shape. He'd seen the leotards and tights and cutaway T-shirts hanging to dry on the service porch, noticed the stack of exercise videos by the VCR.

And the exercises were working. Her body was slimmer again. It was taking on its former tight contours. Except for her breasts. They were disconcertingly ripe, heavy and fuller than ever because she was nursing Emily.

The maddening changes in his wife's body weren't all Clay had to contend with, either. She was spending more time at the office, as well. While she was there, she seemed to make it her personal mission to single-handedly wreak havoc with his concentration.

Clay found that he couldn't walk into the copier room or look for a file without dreading the possibility that he'd have to confront the sight of her, bent over a table stapling papers together. Or standing on tiptoe reaching into a file drawer, the muscles of her calves flexing in a way that sent his libido into hyperdrive.

And then, in bed at night, he didn't know how he bore it. The warmth and scent of her came at him every time she moved. She was so close, just an arm span away. All he had to do was reach for her.

But he refused to reach for her.

It was pure hell. Sometimes he'd lie there, staring at the ceiling, *scenting* her and *knowing* that he wasn't going to last a split second longer. That he was going to roll over and grab her, pull her beneath him and shove himself into her without any preliminary at all.

He'd grit his teeth and turn away, to the very far edge of his side of the bed. He'd think of the shirts he needed laundered, his least favorite client, *anything* to reduce his state of total arousal.

Sometimes Emily, who was now sleeping in her own room, would start to cry. Clay always sighed with relief when that happened.

"I'll go," he'd whisper.

He'd slide out of the bed and pull on his terry robe over the pajama bottoms he slept in nowadays. He'd slip over to the little room next door.

And there he'd find a brief peace, even if it turned out, as it usually did, that Emily was hungry and he couldn't give her what she wanted. There was still that first moment, when he bent over the crib and she blinked and focused in on him, forgetting to wail for an instant.

"What's the problem here?" he would ask.

She'd wail again, flailing her little arms that had grown so fat and round.

He'd pick her up, put her to his shoulder. Every once in a while, that would do it. She'd let out a little burp and snuggle against his neck. But even if burping her didn't work, there was still the chance that changing her was all she needed.

In any case, if she didn't need to be fed, he could sit for a few minutes in the rocker that Granny Sid's mother had brought from the old country. He could hold Emily close and look at the moon out the window.

He could whisper to her how it would be for her, how she would learn to crawl, to walk and to talk. How she'd go to school and take gymnastics or play soccer or maybe even the violin. And how he and her mother would always be there, to teach her about the world and to see that nothing ever harmed her.

Those moments alone with Emily held the greatest peace Clay had ever known. Right now, Emily's wants were so simple, so pure. Food, a dry diaper and a caring touch. Clay could give her those things without much effort at all. Loving Emily was the easiest thing he'd ever done in his life.

Just as what he shared with Emily's mother was the hardest.

* * *

The first storm of the season came on a night in late October, nine weeks after Emily's birth.

That night had been a tough one. Another of those nights when Clay lay in bed awake, wanting his wife and yet somehow managing to hold himself away from her.

The gathering storm outside made it all the worse. There was so much electricity in the air, such a heavy *waiting* feeling. Storms always made him want to break free of all the controls he normally put on himself.

After the first few thunderclaps, he'd heard Emily's cry. Andie had stirred. He'd told her to go back to sleep. And he'd come in here, to hold Emily and soothe both her and himself.

He'd rocked Emily and told her all about storms, how he loved them, how one of his two mothers, whose name had been Rita, had loved them, as well. He whispered what he remembered of Rita in the red coat, turning in circles beneath a downpour. He'd said that storms were nothing to be afraid of. A good storm was one of the best things in life.

Now, Emily was asleep over his shoulder. Clay could feel her stillness, the evenness of her breath moving in and out of her little chest.

Outside, rain lashed the window and the sky lit up. Emily didn't even flinch when the thunder crashed.

Slowly, Clay stood from the rocker. He went to the crib and laid the sleeping child down. She cuddled right up, never stirring, as he covered her with the blankets and tucked her in.

He stood watching her through three more thunderclaps. But she simply went on sleeping. Her little body didn't so much as twitch.

Clay tiptoed back to his own room. But when he got there, he couldn't quite bring himself to climb into the bed beside Andie.

He was drawn to the glass door on which the rain was beating, to beyond that door, where the wind and lightning and thunder ruled. He spared a glance for Andie. She seemed to be sound asleep.

And the storm was pulling at him, inviting him out into it. He went, padding across the floor like a man in a trance.

But he was careful. He slid the door open as smoothly as he could, just wide enough that he could slip through. And he closed it all the way behind him so no icy drafts would wake his wife.

The storm embraced him. He went to the edge of the deck and turned his face to the sky.

In the bed alone, Andie slowly sat up.

She knew where her husband was. She had heard his return, knew that he stood by the bed, felt his hesitation as the storm beckoned to him.

The storm had won. Now he was out in it.

A feeling of sweet anticipation rose inside her. It tingled along each and every one of her nerves.

She probably shouldn't . . .

Yet when it came to Clay, Andie really had no shame.

She threw back the covers and flew to the bathroom where her clumsy fingers almost defeated her in the insertion of her new contraceptive device. But at last she succeeded. The darn thing was in.

Andie looked at herself in the mirror, a shadowed form. She hadn't dared to turn on the light. It was just possible that Clay might have noticed if she had, since there was one high window over the bathtub that looked out on the deck where he now stood.

Andie wore a modest cotton gown with a button front. The gown was perfect for a nursing mother, but not so great for what she had in mind. She gathered up the hem and pulled the gown over her head, dropping it to the tiles at her feet.

She looked at the dark shape of herself in the mirror. Naked, slim, her hair a black cloud. Her breasts were very full. Her milk could come, she knew, if he kissed her in a certain way. She felt the heat in her cheeks at the thought.

But it couldn't be helped. And surely women had made love with their men for century upon century with milk in their breasts. She'd just have to deal with it when and if the moment came.

On the counter not too far from the sink, there was a monitor, as there was in the master bedroom and in all the major rooms of the house. The monitor picked up noises from the baby's room. It was blessedly quiet right then. And Clay had just been in to check on Emily. The chances of her daughter's interrupting them were minimal.

Andie's heart was beating very fast. What if he rejected her? What if she walked out on that deck stark naked and he turned her away?

Oh, that would be terrible.

But she couldn't let herself think that way. If she thought that way she'd give up trying and worse things might happen if she gave up trying. Sweet Lord, he might never make love with her again.

That awful thought mobilized her. She went out of the bathroom and across the floor of the bedroom. At the glass door, she hesitated, pressing her face against the glass to look for him.

She saw him at the railing. He wore his robe and his pajama bottoms, both of which were wet through and clinging to his broad back, his hard, strong legs. He stood with his face turned up, transfixed, beneath the angry sky. His proud, tall body yearned toward the roiling clouds.

Andie's own body relaxed as she watched him. In the space of an instant, everything was changed. All her little fears of rejection, of embarrassment, faded to nothing. The world shimmered under the onslaught of the storm. And she herself was shimmering, needful, hungry for the man outside.

Andie slid the door open, not even bothering to turn and close it behind her. The storm attacked her, pelting her naked body, raising the goose bumps on every inch of her skin.

It was glorious. She lifted her hair and shook it so it fell down her back. And then she tipped her face up, as Clay was doing, letting the rain wash over her, drenching her hair, running down her body in a thousand tiny streams.

When she lowered her face, he was looking at her. His face was naked, washed clean of all pretense. She saw in it the hunger that answered her own.

He said her name, a low, needful sound. And then he covered the distance between them in three long, urgent strides.

Chapter Fifteen

Clay caught Andie's face in his cold wet hands. "You're insane."

"Yes."

"You'll catch pneumonia."

"Or you." She rose on tiptoe, offering her mouth. "Maybe I'll catch you."

He muttered something she didn't really hear, though his meaning was plain. And then he gave her what she craved: his mouth on hers, his tongue delving, his hands everywhere.

Andie held nothing back. She surged up against him, her own hands clutching, grabbing, pushing at his sodden robe. Clay understood what she wanted and helped her, yanking at the soggy terry cloth, shrugging it off, fumbling with the tie of his pajamas and then shoving them down. And at last he was naked, too. No stitch of clothing kept their bodies apart.

The sky opened wider, the rain came down in sheets. Lightning blazed across the heavens and thunder claimed the hills with its roar.

Clay reached down, his wet hands sliding over her, his fingers closing around her thighs from behind. He lifted her, raising her high, sliding her soft, heavy breasts against his chest and then, slowly, he lowered her onto him.

Andie was ready, had been ready forever, it seemed. Clay slipped into her heat and wetness in one smooth, masterful stroke.

She tossed back her head so the water beat on her face. She felt the heavy, sodden coils of her own hair, like silky ropes as they trailed down her back.

"Wrap your legs around me." Clay's voice was harsh, guttural with need.

Andie did as he commanded, encircling him with her thighs, hooking her feet together at the small of his back. Clay staggered away from the railing, clutching her as she clutched him.

And then he turned. Andie felt her back meet the smooth outer wall of the house. Clay used the wall, bracing her against it as he moved in and out of her in long, deep strokes.

Such a sweet, fierce agony, Andie thought in a shattered sort of way. Different than when she'd been pregnant. Now he could be less careful, now he could give the wildness free rein. He seemed to be reaching way up into her, to the very center of her. And she was taking him, all of him, so deep and so good.

Her back scraped the streaming wall. She didn't care. She pushed herself against him, moaning, giving herself up to him. It was a total surrender—one in which he also succumbed.

She stroked his dripping hair, his neck, his shoulders, which bunched and knotted with the strain of keeping her writhing body in place. Everywhere she touched him, the rain ran down in rivulets, making him slick and cold, so hard, so very male.

Lightning flashed again. Thunder clapped.

And then it started.

Her climax came reeling out from that deep place that he was filling so totally. Like a live thing, a flower of sensation, it opened, unfurling petals of wonder along every nerve.

Andie called Clay's name, clutching him even closer, though that didn't seem possible since she held him so tight already. He pressed up, even harder than before. And she felt him spilling as his body jerked and stiffened.

He buried his head against her shoulder. Then he threw it back and groaned his release at the black, roiling sky.

Andie held on, taking all that he gave her, aftertremors shaking her as he finished at last.

And then, the storm still raging around them, they clung to each other, resting against the wall. His head was tucked into the curve of her shoulder, his mouth open against her neck. He kissed her neck, a suckling kind of kiss, as if he could draw back from the pulsing artery there the strength he'd expended in the ecstasy they'd just shared.

Andie twined her fingers in his soaking hair and gave a tug. He groaned as his mouth lost its hold on her flesh. She nuzzled his chin, seeking and at last finding his lips.

The kiss was soft and wet, an endless, tender thing. A caress of aftermath, of fulfillment found, of mutual gratitude at the release that had finally come after these endless weeks of abstinence and denial.

Clay's thighs were quivering; his whole body shook. Andie shook with him. She started to loosen her grip, to slide to the deck floor and relieve him of her weight.

But he grunted a protest into her open mouth. And then he hoisted her, getting a better grip. She instinctively clutched him tighter with her legs. He carried her, reeling more than walking, through the open glass door and back into their bedroom.

He hovered there, by the door, his mouth still locked with hers. She understood what he wanted.

Awkwardly, almost toppling them, she managed to reach out and push the door shut. The keening wind and the beating of the rain receded. When thunder boomed out again, it was muffled, farther away.

Now their breathing and their sighs were the loudest things. The whole dark room was alive with the sounds of their loving. Andie gripped his big shoulders again, wrapped herself around him like ivy on a wall. He took her to the bed, turned and dropped to a sitting position, his feet on the floor.

Now she straddled his lap, facing him, her legs still encircling him. They remained joined, though he was softer inside her. If she lifted just a little, he would slip out.

But he didn't slip out. The kiss went on and on.

He only broke it to nuzzle his way down her cheek, over her jaw, back to her neck and the hot pulse there. His hands came between them. He touched her breasts.

They were hard and full. She knew her milk must be coming, at least a little. But they were both so wet, anyway, it hardly seemed to matter. She didn't even bother to look down and see if it was so.

Clay kissed her neck, licking and sucking, as he fondled her breasts, making them ache and yearn. Down inside her, where he was cuddled limp and safe, she felt herself readying again. And he responded, he grew and hardened, rising, eager for more.

And then he fell backward. He moved up onto the bed, so she could ride him.

And ride him she did. A long, slow time.

It seemed as if this pleasure, this glory, might never have an end. And Andie didn't want it to end. Because now, joined as they were, she could forget all the ways they were so far apart. Here, right now, Clay was open to her. He held nothing back. All the hurts and resentments fled away. No walls existed. They were truly one.

Fulfillment overtook her again, high and pure. Andie rode him harder as it claimed her. And again, as before, he answered with a culmination of his own.

When it was over that time, she fell across him. He stroked her back and coiled her wet hair around his hand.

"Andie, oh, Andie," he breathed against her cheek. "What is it? What is it you do to me?" He sounded lost, almost, and drained and a little sad.

Andie pulled back enough to meet his eyes through the gloom. "I just love you, Clay. That's all. Since the first night you brought me to this house, that's all I've ever done."

He sighed and rolled his head to the side, a gentle rejection of her heartfelt words.

She wouldn't have that. Couldn't bear that. Not after the shattering intimacy they had just shared.

She grabbed his chin in her hand. "Don't do that. Don't turn away from me."

Clay gave in to the pressure of her grip and turned to face her again. But then his strong hand closed around her wrist. "Let go."

Hurt welled in her, sharp and acrid, burning her throat like smoke. This was the ultimate proof of the unscalable wall between them. That he could climb to the heights of heaven with her one moment, and then turn away at the merest mention of the word *love*.

Andie did as he demanded, letting go and sliding off his body at the same time.

"Look, Andie—"

"No." She kept on moving, right off the side of the bed and onto her feet. "Don't say anything more. Please."

"Damn it, Andie..."

She didn't stay to hear the rest. She whirled and made for the bathroom.

She didn't quite make it. Clay got there right behind her and slid in front of the door so she couldn't slam it in his cold, hard face.

Thwarted, Andie glared at him for a moment. Then she drew in a breath, squared her shoulders and flicked on the light. Both of them flinched at the sudden, glaring brightness.

The moment her eyes adjusted, Andie marched to the bathtub, bent, engaged the drain lock and turned on the taps. She poured in some bath salts and watched them foam and bubble.

Clay remained in front of the door, leaning there insolently. Even though she was turned away from him, Andie could feel his exasperation with her. Resentment came off him in waves.

"This is ridiculous," he said at last. "I knew you would do this. The minute I touch you again, you're on me. And when I don't respond the way you think I should, you stage a stupid, childish little tantrum."

She whirled on him. "Fine, Clay. Call it that. Cut me to the heart and then, when I get mad about it, call it a tantrum. And call the love we have nothing more than sex. Do whatever you have to do to keep me on the other side of that wall you've put up."

"You always exaggerate. I've hardly *cut you to the heart*. And if I'm wary of you, well, I'd say with all that's happened, I have a right to be wary."

"Fine. So let's talk about it."

"I told you—"

"I know, I know. No talk. None of that. Never again." She spat the words at him, then turned to climb into the tub.

He grabbed her arm. "Damn you. What the hell do you want from me?"

She looked at his fingers, where they pressed into her tender skin. And then she looked right in his eyes. "I've told you all along what I want. Honesty. And love. It's kind of funny, when you think about it. Since those are the two things you refuse to give me."

He had loosened his grip on her arm a little, but now he squeezed tight again. "I've been truthful with you."

"Have you?"

"You're damn right I have. And you've always known what I think about love. It's a word, and that's all. It's what people *do* that really counts."

"If it's only what people *do* that matters, Clay, then why are you letting us be torn apart?"

"I'm not letting that happen. You're the one who won't—"

"Oh, stop it. Be honest, please, since you keep insisting that you are. Admit to me that all the time now, you're wondering if I'm still carrying a torch for your dead friend."

That did it. He dropped her arm as if it were red-hot. "I'm not wondering anything of the kind."

"Liar." Now she was the one advancing on him. "You are. Admit it."

"I mean it, Andie. Stop this now."

"I won't. No. I won't stop." She had him right up against the door and she spoke directly into his suddenly pale face. "Oh, I know you, Clay Barrett. And I know the lies you tell yourself. Like you don't care about love, love doesn't matter. You're too down-to-earth and realistic for love. And therefore, it shouldn't make any difference if I *think* I love your dead friend. As long as I do what I should do as your wife and Emily's mom. But it *does* make a difference to you, Clay. It's eating you up inside. And until you admit it matters and we can talk about it, we'll just go on being miserable and making each other miserable. And eventually, if you haven't already, you'll start thinking that maybe we'd be better off apart. And then we'll end up—"

"Enough!" The word was a raw, hard shout. He lifted a hand and pushed her gently back from him. "That's not going to happen," he said in a hoarse whisper. "You're my wife, and you'll stay my wife."

Andie shook her head. "Never say never, Clay." All the sorrow of the world was in her voice. "I won't be miserable for the rest of my life. Not even for you."

Right then, from the monitor on the counter, there came a long, angry wail.

Clay sighed. "I'll go."

"No." Andie turned and spun the taps again, this time to the Off position. "I'm sure this time it's food she wants. And anyway, it's my turn." Bending, Andie scooped up the gown she'd left on the floor before she'd followed Clay out into the storm. She pulled it over her head and smoothed it down.

Clay said nothing more as she stepped around him and headed for Emily's room.

The next morning, after Clay left for the office, Andie went out on the deck and found his sodden robe and pajamas. She bent to pick them up and then just stayed there, in a crouch, crying in deep, wrenching sobs.

When the sobs finally tapered off to hiccups and sighs, Andie took the wet things and went inside to put them in the washer. She told herself that maybe she'd feel better now, after having indulged in a good, full-out crying jag.

But she didn't feel better. Especially not when she went to the office and Clay treated her as if he could hardly remember her name.

For the next two weeks, it went on like that. They were like strangers forced to share a life. Andie, not knowing how to reach him, began treating him just as he treated her: with extreme caution.

They were polite and considerate with each other, elaborately so. When they passed each other things at the table, they were scrupulously careful to observe the amenities, to say "please" and "thank you" and "if you wouldn't mind."

Like children who had misbehaved and now wished to show how truly good they could be, they informed each other of their every move.

"I thought I'd go over to the supermarket now."

"Yes, of course. Good idea. Go ahead."

Or...

"Dad wants to play golf this afternoon. I was thinking I'd join him at the course."

"Yes, that's fine. Why don't you, then?"

"I will. I'll do that."

"Good. That's just fine."

It was awful. Andie felt that she lived in some artificial world. A perfect world, where no true emotions were allowed to sully the plastic purity of it all.

It was so bad, so banal, so utterly unreal, that Andie almost found herself regretting what she and Clay had shared on the night of the storm. She almost wished she could turn back the clock, let Clay go out on the deck into the storm alone and stay in bed herself.

Because if they hadn't made love in that shattering, total way, she probably never would have said the things she'd said later. She might have kept to herself those painful truths, truths that cut so close to the bone that now Clay wouldn't come near her, much less take her in his arms.

Each day, Andie woke positive that it couldn't go on like this. Something would happen to turn things around.

But each day would slide by, artificial and stifling as ever.

She talked to Ruth Ann. Ruth Ann said she had to keep trying.

So she did, she tried again, though she felt battered and bloody from all the trying she'd done.

It was Friday night and they were watching television.

"Clay. Clay, could we turn this off?"

"What for?"

"Clay, we need to talk."

He looked at her. A look of such weary patience that all her will to confront him faded to nothing.

She couldn't do it. She was as tired of it as he was. "Never mind," she said.

They watched the rest of the program and then went to bed.

And bed was the worst of all. In bed there were miles, continents, between them.

Andie had a premonition that the day would come when Clay would begin to sleep in one of the spare rooms. He'd wait for some reasonable excuse, of course. That he was keeping her up with his reading, which he often stayed up late to do. Or maybe he'd catch a cold and decide he was disturbing her with his coughing and sniffling. He'd move to another room. And never move back.

Andie thought, *This is how it happens between men and women. The love is there, but some hard truth can't be faced. They live a lie with each other. And all the warmth and closeness slowly dries up and blows away.*

Two weeks after the storm, Andie knew she wouldn't be able to bear this forever. She simply would not become a dried-up woman, living an empty life beside a cold, distant man.

She was better off alone.

It hurt, just thinking it. But sometimes the truth hurt.

She wasn't yet to the point where she was ready to take action. She wasn't ready to pack her suitcase or consider the awful effect her leaving might have on Emily. She wasn't even ready to start scanning Apartment For Rent ads.

But the idea was in her mind. The idea was like a tiny seed that had found fertile soil in the cold silence that lay between herself and her husband. A little sprout was unfurling from the seed, though no one could see it yet; it was still underground.

Soon, Andie started thinking to herself. Soon something has to give.

On the second Friday in November, Andie and Clay sat in the family room after Emily was in bed. Clay read a spy novel.

Andie did nothing. She leaned back in her big comfortable chair and closed her eyes.

She thought about how normal they would look to any outsider. A lovely young couple relaxing on a Friday night from the fulfilling demands of their new family and their growing business.

She glanced over at Clay. He was a handsome, successful man. And to any casual observer, she would appear to be his female counterpart. They had a beautiful daughter, a wonderful home. And Barrett & Co. was doing just fine. They had it all.

But together, just the two of them alone, they had nothing. Nothing but walls and distance and lies.

The doorbell rang, cutting through her grim thoughts.

Clay glanced up from his book. "Who's that?"

Andie shrugged. "I don't know."

"Do you want me to get it?"

Andie pushed herself out of the deep, soft chair. "No. Read your book. I'll see who it is."

Andie walked down the hall to the front door, her mind on the walls that were unscalable, the distance so vast it had become immeasurable. And the lies. The lies that were sacred now. Never to be disturbed.

Something has to happen, Andie thought for the hundredth time. She turned the handle and pulled back the door.

Madeline Kirkland was waiting on the other side.

Chapter Sixteen

Madeline shivered a little and stuck her hands deeper into the pockets of her expensive trench coat. "I would have called. But I was afraid you wouldn't see me. So I found my way out here. I figured I'd be harder to say no to face-to-face."

Andie only stared, thinking that Madeline looked thinner, and that she'd cut her hair.

"You look...thinner," Madeline said.

"I was just thinking the same thing about you."

Madeline glanced away, into the darkness beyond the porch, and then back. "Your baby?"

"She was a little early. But she's fine."

"A girl, then?"

"Yes. We named her Emily."

"Emily. I like that." Somewhere off in the oaks, an owl hooted.

"Well?" A laugh that sounded a little like a sob escaped Jeff's widow. "May I come in?"

Andie stepped back. "Yes, of course."

"Is Clay here?"

"Yes, he's here."

"I want... I must talk with you. With both of you."

"All right." Andie closed the door and gestured toward the family room. "Through that way."

Madeline turned where Andie pointed.

"Wait."

Madeline froze, then looked back, a question in her eyes.

"Your coat," Andie said lamely. "Why don't you give it to me and I'll hang it up?"

"Oh. Certainly." Madeline took off the coat and handed it over. Then she squared her shoulders and headed toward the family room.

Clay looked up when he heard the sound of high-heeled shoes on the hall floor.

When Madeline appeared, he stared, just as Andie had done. "Madeline?"

"Yes. It's me." She stood awkwardly before him.

He swallowed. Dread curled in his stomach.

Andie appeared from the hall. "Madeline wants to talk with us, Clay."

"What about?" He tried not to sound harsh, but somehow it came out that way.

Madeline said softly, "I think you know."

Clay set his book down. He understood the urge trapped animals had, to chew off their own limbs in order to escape. But Clay wasn't an animal. He looked from Madeline's grim, set face to Andie's and then he tried one last time to avoid the inevitable. "Are you sure this is necessary?"

"Yes," Madeline said.

"All right."

There was an agonized silence, then Andie indicated the couch. "Please. Sit down. Can I get you something? Coffee? Are you hungry?"

Madeline sat and shook her head. "Nothing. Really. I'm fine."

Andie sank into the chair she'd left when she answered the door.

Madeline said, "Oh. This is difficult. I don't know quite where to begin."

"Just do it," Andie said. "Start anywhere."

"All right, I…Jeff never balanced his checkbook." Clay stared at Madeline, wondering what in the hell Jeff's checkbook had to do with anything. Madeline went on. "Just think of that. I probably never would have figured out the truth if he hadn't turned over all the money matters to me when we got married."

Beside Clay, Andie made a little noise, a sound of dawning awareness. "You found the canceled check."

Madeline nodded. "I found a check he wrote to someone named Andrea McCreary. I never connected the name with you, Andie, because I don't think anyone had ever mentioned your last name. And Clay never called you Andrea—that I remember. It was always Andie, when he talked about you. But anyway, I found a check for five thousand dollars made out to someone I'd never heard of named Andrea McCreary. I asked Jeff about it. He gave me some story about splitting a commission with another real estate agent. The story didn't make a lot of sense to me, but I let it go. After all, it was a check he had written *before* we were married and how he spent his money then wasn't really any of my business. But it bothered me. It stayed there, unresolved, in the back of my mind."

Madeline looked at Clay. "I didn't put it together until Andie said her maiden name the day of the funeral. And at that moment, it all made hideous sense. The check. And the

way you came that day at the very end of February, Clay.
You went off with Jeff and he came back with his face all
battered. He said you two had been mugged. But of course
you'd had a fight with each other, right?''

Gruffly, he answered her. "Yeah."

"And then there were the half-truths you told me, about
Andie being pregnant already when you got married. I assumed you meant she was pregnant by *you,* but you never
actually said that in so many words. And then you said
you'd never contacted Jeff and me again because you were
so wrapped up in your new life. Well, of course, I'm sure
that was part of it. But the main reason was that you and
Jeff had agreed never to see each other again. Isn't that
so?"

"Yeah. It's so."

"I knew it. I knew it all, at that moment when Andie said
her maiden name. I saw the truth. And I couldn't face it.
Not then, anyway."

Madeline's hand lay along the arm of the couch. She
moved it to her lap to join her other hand. She looked down
at her folded hands. Clay thought she appeared very de-
mure, almost schoolgirlish, sitting that way, with her slim
legs pressed so close together and both of her feet placed
primly on the floor.

But then she looked up and he saw a grown woman's agony in her eyes. "But now I see that I *have* to face the truth.
That I can't go on without knowing for sure."

Madeline dragged in a breath, looked down at her hands
again. "Jeff was . . . well, you know how he was. He lit up
a room when he entered it, but he often left disaster in his
wake. When I married him, I knew what he was like. And
I accepted him just as he was. We'd grown up together and
I . . . I understood him. He was an only child and his parents spoiled him—and yet also expected so much of him.
He could never live up to what they wanted. And then they

both died, before he'd come to any sort of peace with them. He was . . ."

Madeline seemed not to know how to go on. She put her hands to her cheeks, as if to steady the thoughts inside her head. Then she folded her hands in her lap once more and took another long breath. "I guess what I mean is, I *knew* Jeff. I never knew anyone the way I knew him. There was such intimacy between us. And yet—he feared our closeness. Sometimes he'd run away from it. But for me, there was just never anyone else. I could never imagine a world without him in it. But now I have to do more than imagine it. I have to *live* with it. I have to make my own peace with Jeff's memory and go on."

Madeline turned to Andie. "That's why I have to know. I can't seem to get on with my life until I know."

Andie said softly, "It's all right. I understand."

And Madeline asked the question at last. "Is your baby my husband's child?"

Clay felt as if someone had punched him in the gut.

But Andie looked so calm.

And when she spoke, her voice was as composed as her expression. "In all the ways that matter," she said, "Clay is Emily's father. He's the one who's been there from the first. And Emily already knows how important he is in her life." Andie smiled, a bemused, wondering smile. "If you could just see her face, when she hears his voice or when he bends over her crib and she can make out his features. She looks so...happy, so totally trusting and content, when she recognizes him. She's a lucky little girl. To have a dad like Clay."

Andie sat forward a little in her chair. "But I'm not answering the question the way you meant it, I know. And so I'll tell you this. Yes, I spent one night with Jeff Kirkland during the holidays last year. I found out, after it was too late, that Jeff was only trying to forget how much he was missing *you*. It was a . . . foolish act, by two foolish people. And it had consequences.''

"You became . . . pregnant.'' Madeline's voice broke on the last word.

"Yes. I became pregnant by Jeff. But I was fortunate. Clay found out and wanted to marry me. So it turned out that Emily got a real father, after all.''

Madeline's clasped hands were white at the knuckles, though her face was composed. She coughed. "I see.''

No one seemed to know what to say then. Silence echoed in the room.

Madeline opened the small purse she carried and lifted out a handkerchief. She dabbed at her upper lip with it before she went on in a clipped tone. "There's something else. One more thing. There's money from the Kirkland trust for the baby. For Emily. I would be glad to arrange for that money to be put aside for her.''

Andie turned then, to look at Clay. "What do you think?''

Clay didn't know what he thought. The world seemed to have spun right off its axis and whirled into a whole new dimension. He was still reeling from the way Andie was dealing with all this. She had so serenely described him as Emily's true father. And she'd mentioned Jeff so frankly and dispassionately—as if she was completely over him, as if whatever she might have shared with him was long, long in the past.

"Clay?'' Andie prompted.

Clay did his best to collect his scattered wits. It seemed only fitting that he should approach this situation fairly and rationally—as both Andie and Madeline seemed to be doing. "Well, I think when she's old enough, she should probably be told something about Jeff. And I think it would be right for Jeff to have left her some money.''

"All right, then," Madeline said. She stood. "We don't have to go into the particulars of it now, I don't think. But it should be set up so Emily can claim the money when she reaches her majority. And of course the money should also be available for her education."

"Yes," Clay said. "That sounds right."

Andie urged, "Madeline. Stay awhile."

Clay blinked. He wasn't catching on too fast here. He hadn't realized that Madeline was ready to go. But now he could see that she meant to leave right away.

"No." Madeline opened her purse again, put her handkerchief away. "I can't. Not now. I need some time. This was hard. Please understand."

"Yes," Andie said. "We do. We understand. Maybe later, then..."

"Yes," Madeline agreed. "Maybe later. I think someday I'd like that."

Andie rose to her feet and Clay, feeling slow and confused, followed suit. They trailed behind Madeline to the front door, with Andie stopping at the coat closet to retrieve Madeline's coat.

Moments later, Madeline had disappeared down the gravel walk to the driveway. Andie closed the door and leaned back against it.

Clay stared at her, feeling as if he was seeing her for the very first time. Damned if he didn't admire what he saw. "You said we'd be hearing from her again."

"Yes. I did." She pushed herself away from the door. "All at once, I'm beat."

"I know what you mean."

"I think I'll go on upstairs. Will you turn off the lights when you come?"

"Sure. No problem."

Andie left Clay standing there, left him wondering what in the world to do next.

He watched her climbing the stairs. She held on to the banister the whole way, her exhaustion clear in every line of her slim form.

Eventually, Clay shook himself. He went to the family room and turned off the lights. Then he, too, mounted the stairs.

He checked on Emily. She was sleeping peacefully. He couldn't resist touching her hand. As always, she curled her fingers around his. She gave a little sigh and a trace of a smile curled her tiny mouth.

Emily was a happy baby. She trusted her world and the people in it. So far, Clay realized, he'd done right by his daughter.

But he couldn't be so proud of himself when it came to her mother.

"There was such intimacy between us," Madeline had said about her relationship with Jeff. "And yet—he feared our closeness. Sometimes he'd run away from it...."

Clay sank to the rocker by Emily's crib. It hurt to think of Madeline's words. They were too true. And not only in reference to Madeline and Jeff.

What was that other thing Madeline had said?

It was so close to what Andie had said on the night before Jeff's funeral. That she and Clay had to face the truth between them. They had to drag it into the light and see it for what it was.

Slowly, Clay rose from the rocker. He could hide here in the baby's room no longer. He went looking for his wife.

Chapter Seventeen

Andie was in the shower. Clay could hear the water running behind the closed door of the bathroom.

He sank to the edge of the bed, facing the closed door. He was still sitting there in the same place ten minutes later when his wife emerged wrapped in her robe, rubbing the wet strands of her hair with a towel.

Andie paused there, in the doorway to the bathroom. "Clay? Are you all right?"

"I don't know." He stared at her, and then put his head in his hands and gazed blindly down at the floor between his knees. "I..."

Andie approached the bed, the fabric of her robe whispering as her bare legs moved. Once there, she sank down beside him. "Clay?"

He lifted his head again and looked at her. She was so beautiful, with her shower-pink skin, her wet, shining hair. "Andie, I...I want to ask you..."

"Yes?"

"God. I don't know where to begin."

He watched the hope leap into her eyes. It was so bright that it nearly blinded him.

"It doesn't matter. Begin anywhere." Her voice was carefully controlled. She didn't want to jump to conclusions—he could see that. And yet she sensed what was happening. At last, the moment when he would be honest with her had come.

"I...I've been losing you, haven't I? Little by little, every day."

She nodded. She was biting her lip, her eyes glittering with unshed tears.

"Are you gone all the way yet? Is there any chance that—?"

She could control herself no longer. "Oh, Clay, yes. Of course there's a chance. When there's love, there's always a chance."

"What do I have to do?"

She wiped her eyes with her towel. "You mean this? You really want to know?"

"Yeah. I mean it."

"All right. I'll tell you. You have to ask me that awful question you're so afraid to ask. You have to get it out in the open so we can deal with it."

He looked at her for a moment more. The temptation was very great to pretend he didn't know what question she meant. But then he thought of Madeline. Her life had been shattered, yet still she came around. She sought the truth.

If Madeline could do it, so could he.

He asked the question, "Do you still love him? Do you still love Jeff?"

"At last," she murmured in a wondering voice.

"Well. Do you?"

"I never loved him." Her eyes were brimming again. There was such joy in her face. "I told you months ago I didn't. And I was telling the truth."

Clay was silent. Then he admitted, "I don't...know how to do this, to talk about the things that hurt. Until I was ten, nobody would listen. And then Dad and Mom took me in. They respected my habit of silence. I learned to *do,* and let my actions speak for me."

Andie set her towel aside and reached for his hand, enfolding it in her two softer ones. "I understand, Clay. I really do. And maybe that worked out pretty well, when there was only you. But now, there are the two of us—the three of us, including Emily. And we can't live this way, with all these unsaid things between us. We need to talk about them." She looked down at their hands and then back up at him. "Can we talk now, Clay? Please? Can I tell you all about it? About what an idiot I was, and why it happened, and *how* it happened?"

Clay moved the hand she clasped, enough so that their fingers could entwine. "Yes. Yes, I suppose you'd better," he said. "Talk to me, Andie. Tell me. All of it."

The words came tumbling out.

"It started when you returned from L.A., really. When you came home to take over the business..."

She told him how she'd felt then, so edgy and unsatisfied, yet unable to let her feelings out because she was determined to prove to him that she deserved her job.

"I thought if you ever got wind of how frustrated I was with having to show *you,* of all people, that I was really good at my job, you'd fire me on the spot."

Clay couldn't help admitting, "I might have. At first."

"Exactly. Anyway, I got through those months when you first came back. Things were going better. I knew you'd started to realize that I was an asset to Barrett and Company. Then Jeff came. And he was bright and fun and easy to be with. I understood he'd had some sort of problem, that he'd broken off an engagement. But I didn't really give it a lot of thought. I wasn't really *after* him or anything. I just liked him. He was fun to be around. And then New Year's Eve came. We all went to Ruth Ann and Johnny's. You were dating Jill Peters, remember?''

He thought of Jill, though it was hard to picture her face. "Yes. I remember."

"Anyway, that night it seemed like everyone in the world was coupled up. Except me and Jeff. You and Jill left early."

"She had to work the next day."

"Whatever. You two left early. And I...I imagined that you were going somewhere to be alone together. I suppose I was jealous, though I didn't know it then."

"You were...?"

"Let me finish."

"All right."

"I drank more champagne. And Jeff and I kissed when the clock struck twelve. And he took me home, because I'd had more champagne than I should have. At my apartment, I had another bottle of champagne in the fridge. We opened it. We started talking. And I told him my dream."

"Your dream?"

For the first time, Andie looked away. But after a moment, she collected herself and went on. "Yes. I'd always dreamed that there would be this man. And I'd know him when I saw him. And that we'd make love and it would be wonderful and we'd be together for the rest of our lives."

Andie swallowed. "Jeff was great, he really was. I mean, he didn't laugh at me. He just listened. I started out talking about my dream as if it was something that didn't really matter anymore. I was trying to be sophisticated—you know, a worldly woman who was through with all that girlish sentimental stuff. Jeff and I even shared a toast—to the death of my silly romantic dreams. But then, when I lowered my glass after the toast, I just burst into tears. I was sobbing and sniffling. And I said, 'Oh, Jeff. There isn't going to be any special man, I know that now. It's just a fantasy. And I've been waiting all my life for someone who doesn't exist.'

"Jeff was holding me by then, kind of rubbing my back. My head was bowed, but then I lifted it to look in his eyes. We stared at each other for a moment. And then he kissed me. And after that, it just happened. We lay back on the couch and fumbled with our clothes. And we...had sex. It was awkward and painful—for me at least. And I don't think it was much different for Jeff. And when it was over, we both started apologizing to each other."

Andie gave a wrenching little laugh. "It still amazes me. That from an act so...grim and mechanical, something like Emily came." Andie clutched Clay's hand tightly. The tears still glittered in her eyes. One ran over the rim of her lower lid and trailed down her cheek to drop on their clasped hands. "Oh, Clay. It was such a stupid, reckless act. You can't know the guilt I feel for it. No one can...." Her teeth were clenched. Another tear fell.

Clay pulled her close and rocked her a little, whispering soothing, tender things against her wet hair. Finally, Andie was comforted enough to pull back a little, though she still gripped his hand as if she would never let go.

"And then," she said with a sniffle, "Jeff started talking. He talked about Madeline. I don't really remember exactly what he said. But I could see how much he loved her. And how totally confused he was. And so I called him an idiot. I called him ten kinds of fool. I said, here I was lonely all the time because the love I was waiting for had never come to be. And there *he* was, with exactly the kind of love I would do anything for. And he was throwing it away. I told him to get back to L.A. and get down on his knees and beg that woman to take him back. And he . . . he said that was exactly what he was going to do."

"And he did," Clay said tenderly. "Do you remember that morning when Madeline called to say Jeff was dead?"

Andie shuddered. "I'll never forget it."

"Well, that morning, she thanked me. For whatever I'd said to Jeff over the holidays. She said it had made all the difference. That when Jeff came back, he was changed. He really wanted to marry her then."

Andie's smile was so sad and soft. "She did?"

"Yes, she did. She told me how grateful she was to me. I didn't argue with her. How could I at a time like that? But I had no idea what she was talking about. Now I do, though. It was what *you* had said to him."

Andie didn't completely agree. "I think what really happened was that he had finally figured it out for himself. I only put in words what he'd already decided. But it is strange. Because I've always felt like I owed Jeff a debt, too. Because of him, because of all that happened as a result of that one night, I finally found what I was looking for." She paused for a moment, and then she gave a low, musing laugh.

"What?"

"Just remembering. I was so full of . . . silly fantasies then. I was right about that special man. But I was afraid to admit to myself that he was you. I didn't even know what love was. Until I suddenly had to grow up—and until us."

Clay had to clear his throat before he asked, rather stupidly, "You didn't?"

"No, I didn't. Oh, Clay. When will you let me love you? When will you believe that I do know what love is now, and I love *you*, Clay Barrett, more than anyone in the world . . . except maybe the baby sleeping in the other room?"

Clay took her words into himself. They filled him to overflowing with shining, glorious hope.

But there was another question he'd been holding back, one that had been eating away at him since the day after he found out Jeff Kirkland was dead.

He dared to asked it: "If you love *me,* then why the hell did you insist on going to *his* funeral?"

Andie let out a heartfelt sigh. "How many times do I have to tell you? I went because of *you.* Because I thought you would need me. And I wanted to be there, if you did. I was sure Jeff would never have told Madeline about the baby. So Madeline shouldn't have had a clue that the baby was his. But she did have a clue. She had that canceled check. And so the truth came out, after all. And all the stress made me go into labor. It was so horrible. I knew I'd made one mistake in judgment after another. And yet you kept insisting that it was all right. But it wasn't all right."

"I know," he whispered softly. "I know."

"Oh, Clay. I've been so *lonely.* It's been forever since you've let me near."

"I *couldn't* let you near."

"Why?"

He thought for a moment before he tried to explain. "Remember when you said I had to forgive Jeff and then forgive you, too?"

"Yes."

"Well, you and Jeff weren't the only ones I had to forgive. There was myself, too. I'd called Jeff dead—and then he *was* dead. And I realized I'd turned my back on him."

"But what else could you have done?"

"I don't know. But sometimes I think there might have been a better choice."

"For a saint, maybe. But, Clay, you're just a man."

"I know." He shook his head. "Do I ever know. But it seemed like I had just messed everything up. And I had let you down, don't you see? In the most important way. For all those years, I watched you. I think I always felt that I was watching *out* for you. And then, one night I *didn't* watch out for you. And my own best friend took advantage of you."

"No, that's not true. Or at least if Jeff did take advantage of me, I did exactly the same thing to him. We took advantage of each other that night. And it really wasn't your fault, not in any way." She let out a rueful chuckle. "In fact, when the truth came out, you went far beyond the call of duty. I mean, you married me yourself and gave Emily your own name."

"But if I had only—"

"What? Not gone out with Jill that night so I wouldn't have been so jealous?"

"You're kidding. You weren't really jealous, were you?"

"I didn't know it then. But yes, you're darn right I was."

Clay thought of Jeff again. And it wasn't as painful as it had been. He was able to explain. "All through college, Jeff was my damn *hero*, did you know that? He was the opposite of me. He was like you, always looking for adventure, always ready to have fun."

"And he was reckless and he could be thoughtlessly cruel, as well. And now he's gone. It's so sad." She laid a hand on the side of his face. "But if you want to talk about heroes, then the real hero was right here all along."

Clay captured the hand that caressed his face. "I'm no hero, Andie."

"Yes, yes you are. You're my hero. The best kind of hero. The kind who never rides off into the sunset, the kind who knows how to change a diaper, and load the dishwasher—and hold the baby for two hours while she's screaming with colic. The kind who also just happens to turn my bones to jelly every time you kiss me ..."

"Hell, Andie, I—"

She touched his face again, a tender, knowing touch. "Oh, Clay. Can't you see? It's love, Clay. Love is the thing that binds it all together. Love is the thing that makes forgiveness possible. And if you hold yourself aloof from love, then one wrong move from someone who matters to you, and it all falls apart. If you don't believe I love you, how can you know I mean the best for you, want to be with you, would never hurt you on purpose? None of the important things between a man and a woman can exist without love, Clay. Not trust. Not forgiveness. And not a future."

"What are you telling me?"

"Only what I've been trying to tell you for months. That I love you. With all my heart. In the very special and specific way that a woman loves the only man for her. Won't you please believe me now?"

He let a heartbeat pass before he answered, "Yes."

Clay had never seen a smile as beautiful as the one she gave him then. And then she leaned her head on his shoulder.

He put his arm around her and spoke against her damp, sweet-smelling hair. "Hell, Andie. I have to say it. If there's any hero around here, it's you."

She lifted her head at that and turned to grant him an impudent grin. "You noticed." Lord, she was adorable.

"Andie . . ." He tipped up her chin.

Their lips almost met, but she held back at the last possible second. "Say it."

He faked an innocent look. "What, that you're my hero?"

"You know what. Say it now."

He stroked the curve of her back with the hand that wasn't holding her chin. "I want you. Damn. I always want you."

But that wasn't enough for her. She pushed him away. "Say it, Clay. Say it now."

"Come back here."

"Not until you tell me. Not until you say the words. There are only three—four, including my name. Four simple little words."

"Damn it, Andrea Barrett."

"Those aren't the ones."

He reached for her and caught her. "You're not going to let me off the hook on this, are you?"

"You're right, I'm not."

"All right."

"I'm listening."

He said it, very slowly, so she wouldn't miss a word. "I love you, Andie."

Her smile was as bright as the sun after a wild, dark storm. "And I love you, Clay."

And then there was no more need for words. Their lips met. Their lifetime bond was sealed at last, in the best and truest way—with honesty and love.

* * * * *